THE LEGEND OF STORMY AND THE GREAT NORTHERN CHRISTMAS SPIRIT & TREE COMPANY

Thomas L Jaegly

authorHOUSE

AuthorHouse™
1663 Liberty Drive
Bloomington, IN 47403
www.authorhouse.com
Phone: 1 (800) 839-8640

© 2019 Thomas L Jaegly. All rights reserved.

No part of this book may be reproduced, stored in a retrieval system, or transmitted by any means without the written permission of the author.

Published by AuthorHouse 08/16/2019

ISBN: 978-1-7283-0589-9 (sc)
ISBN: 978-1-7283-0588-2 (hc)
ISBN: 978-1-7283-0590-5 (e)

Library of Congress Control Number: 2019903581

Printed in the United States of America.

Any people depicted in stock imagery provided by Getty Images are models, and such images are being used for illustrative purposes only.
Certain stock imagery © Getty Images.

This book is printed on acid-free paper.

Because of the dynamic nature of the Internet, any web addresses or links contained in this book may have changed since publication and may no longer be valid. The views expressed in this work are solely those of the author and do not necessarily reflect the views of the publisher, and the publisher hereby disclaims any responsibility for them.

If you enjoy this book, consider books 2 and 3 in the series;
Searching for The Great Northern Christmas Spirit & Tree Company and
Saving The Great Northern Christmas Spirit & Tree Company
Both are available on Amazon. (search by title, author or Amazon.com/dp/B0BKGLYFWV)

Chapter 1

"It's tradition." That's one of the answers I often get. "It's tradition." Until recently, that seemed like enough.

I'm thirteen years old now, and "It's tradition" is less of an answer and more of an easy way to keep me from asking more questions—questions that might be difficult for adults to answer. These are the types of questions young children with curious minds and active imaginations always seem to ask. They usually start with a single word like "Why?" and end up with an even simpler answer like "Because" or "I said so" or something even less helpful like "It's tradition."

Well, I have decided to ask those questions and continue to do so until I get past the usual answers. I am going to ask the questions that require adult answers. It's a bold move on my part, especially since it's Christmastime, and I am at my grandma Jane's house.

We have just finished decorating her Christmas tree, and my dad is getting ready to serve the hot cocoa with the little marshmallows. If you knew my grandma, then you would know how bold a move on my part this is going to be. I'm going to question her most precious tradition: putting a reindeer on the top of the Christmas tree. You heard me right. I said a *reindeer* Christmas tree topper. What is even worse is that this isn't just any ordinary reindeer tree topper, as if there were such a thing. This reindeer tree topper has a name: Stormy.

I could almost understand if the reindeer's name was Blitzen or Donner or the name of any of the well-known reindeers associated with

Christmas. But I've never seen this reindeer's name anywhere, except on the top of her Christmas tree.

This reindeer named Stormy isn't found in any of the books I've ever read. I've never seen him in any Christmas cartoons or movies. Heck, I've never even heard him mentioned in any of the Christmas songs, and believe me: we sing a lot of them in this family.

The decision to question the whole Stormy thing is not just bold but epic. It is going to call into question not only the Stormy tree topper tradition but all the Christmas traditions that have been going on in my family since before I was born, even before my dad was born.

Since this is Grandma's *tradition*—and we are at her house, and it's her tree, her decorations, and her topper—I've decided to go straight to the top with my first real adult question and will challenge Grandma herself.

By the way, my name is Brandi, and to pull this off, timing will be everything.

Chapter 2

The hot cocoa is ready. It is not the kind of cocoa you get from the little packs. It isn't from a box that says to add two heaping spoonfuls to one cup of hot water and stir until completely mixed. It's not from a coffee shop at the strip mall, the kind of place with all the fake snow sprayed on the outside windows and "Happy Holidays!" etched into it. And it's not just chocolate milk heated in a Christmas mug in the microwave and sprinkled with marshmallows to look like cocoa. This is real cocoa spooned out of a metal canister that has a round metal lid in the center of the top. The canister looks like it is older than me, older than my dad, and heck, even older than my grandma. This is the same type of metal canister that we have used every year that I can remember. I think that even the same metal spoon has been used to open the metal lid.

The cocoa is not mixed with water or milk and heated up in the microwave. The cocoa is spooned into a big old metal pan full of real cream—thick, sweet cream—and put on the stove at a low heat. The same spoon we use to scoop out the cocoa and put it into the pan is used to stir the contents. The stirring is done at a slow pace with what I would describe as *love*. It is done smoothly in a counterclockwise direction, never the other way, and always with great caution.

My dad is the only one I have ever seen make the cocoa, and no one ever questions it. Before him, I imagine my grandma performed this task. I assume she did it the same way every time, without any variation to this exhaustingly slow, cautious, and loving method he is using right now.

As the thick, sweet smell of the cocoa drifts out of the old metal pan, fanned by the old metal spoon moving in a constant, smooth, and gentle counterclockwise direction, I decide that I'm going to ask the first of what may turn out to be many questions that will bring answers like "Because," "I said so," and "It's tradition." Only this time, I will keep asking these questions until I get real answers.

The answers I'm looking for are the ones my dad must have gotten at some point in his life. The kinds of answers that must change people so deeply they decide to follow this thing called tradition without question or variation. The kinds of answers that must forever change the way a person sees the world.

At thirteen years old, I now want that power. It's time for me to be treated as an adult. All my life, I have been sitting in the background, not quite part of the group. I have always wanted to be accepted as an equal and to participate in the important things I believe make the adults believe they are somehow wiser than us kids. I believe the answers I seek will propel me into a place in life where I will never have to endure these types of answers again; everyone will know I'm ready to hear the truth. I'll be ready to make my own choices and do what I know is right and not just what I'm told to do. My life will finally be easy, and things will go smoothly. No more rules to follow. All I'll have to do is what is right for me.

Yep, this is my time. Today is my day, and I'm ready for the truth.

Chapter 3

Dad announces the cocoa is done, which means we will each get a cup and be given eight miniature marshmallows to put in our mugs—not six, not seven, and not nine or ten. *Eight.*

Once the cocoa is poured and the marshmallows are inserted, we go back into the living room and take seats around the tree.

Dad returns to the stepstool next to the tree one last time and checks that the tree is ready and the special cord used for the tree topper is in the proper place. I guess this all seems like a normal thing when it comes to Christmas tree trimming: generations gathered at Grandma's house, the tree ready to be lit, hot cocoa in hand, the tree topper in place, and the first lighting of the family tree. If all this is normal, then I must let you know that's where normal ends in my family.

It's not the tree itself. The tree is normal enough. It's a real tree. I used to ask my dad what the difference was between a real Christmas tree and a fake one, and he would always say that they were both real trees but only one was alive. Then he would laugh to himself like he'd made a funny Christmas tree joke. He would say a real tree was one grown in the ground and a fake tree was built in a factory. He also said there were two types of real trees: live and cut.

I quit asking.

We always get a live tree for Grandma's house. She always wants a Douglas fir, and it has to be five feet tall from the bottom branches to the top. The live trees are sold with large burlap bags covering their roots. The burlap bags cover the roots and contain dirt from where the trees were dug up. This dirt feeds the trees and keeps them alive. It allows the trees to continue to grow and helps the trees maintain their strong, sweet, evergreen fragrance. I have been told this also allows the tree to be replanted after the Christmas season is over, but up until now, I have never wondered who replants these trees or where they are replanted. This year, I intend to find out.

The cut trees are different from the live trees in that they don't have any roots and are put in a Christmas tree stand to help them stay upright. Most of my friends have this type. The tree stand is filled with water that the tree absorbs through the cut trunk, in an effort to stay alive. Some people put sugar in the water to help feed the tree, and others even put candy canes in the water for the same reason. But usually after a week or so, these cut trees quit absorbing the water and begin to turn brownish. Without the aid of its roots and the dirt, the cut trees start to drop their needles, and most of them even lose their sweet evergreen smell well before the end of the Christmas season. These cut trees end up as firewood or recycled or dragged to the curb in a big white bag, waiting for the garbage truck to haul them away to the dump, along with all the empty boxes and colorful piles of wrapping paper.

My dad and I have the same type of tree as Grandma's at our house, a live tree, for the same reason. Whenever I would ask Dad why our family gets this type of tree and not the cut type, he would always say, "Because it's tradition."

Grandma's tree, its five feet of branches along with the brown bag of roots, make it a total of seven feet tall. Grandma says this is just perfect because she has nine-foot-high ceilings, and it gives Stormy room to stand proud without being too crowded. Yes, like I said before, Stormy is the name of Grandma's tree topper. Don't worry; I'll be getting back to Stormy in due time. He is just one of the many traditions that I will be questioning on this day.

My dad waits patiently on the stool. Grandma reaches into the box that held the decorations and pulls out one last old box. It's about nine inches tall, eleven inches long, and four inches deep and looks as old as the metal cocoa canister. It is made of wood and has a sliding top. On the side of the box is printed in fancy script "The Great Northern

Christmas Spirit & Tree Co." Oddly enough, this is the first time I ever remember reading that logo on the side of the box. It sticks out in my mind because the Great Northern Christmas Spirit & Tree Co. is the name of the place we get our Christmas trees from. This is the first year I remember seeing the sign on the side of the road, an old-looking sign, with the same fancy script and the words "The Great Northern Christmas Spirit & Tree Co." written on it. The sign was in the shape of an arrow, and it pointed down a snow-covered trail into the woods. The trail weaved through the woods for what felt like a couple of miles and ended at a clearing. A tiny cottage sat near the edge of a forest of evergreens.

Another thing that seems odd to me is this is the first year I remember seeing the old gentleman with the red cheeks and the big smile come from the building. This year, I remember the old gentleman coming to our SUV, my dad getting out and shaking his hand like he was a very close friend. This is the first year I remember Dad helping the old gentleman tie the tree to the top of the SUV, thanking him, and wishing him a Merry Christmas.

The old gentleman replied, "Merry Christmas to you, and wish your mom a Merry Christmas from me also."

I'm not sure why, but after that, all I remember is being back on the road and on our way here to Grandma's.

All of the years before this, I guess I must have been asleep as we approached the old sign in the shape of the arrow and turned onto the snow-covered trail that led to the clearing with the old man and the cottage. I must have slept through the tree being hoisted to the top of the SUV.

As Dad took the wooden box from Grandma and slid the top open, I knew my time was near, and timing is everything. I knew the time for me to ask my questions was drawing close.

Dad took Stormy out of the old box, which was as old as the cocoa canister, older than me, or my dad, and maybe even older than Grandma herself, but it still looks like it could be brand new. I guess all the care she takes with it keeps it looking this way. It is always treated gently and never leaves the box, except on December 21. It is only out for a short time, just until New Year's Day, and then it is carefully put back in its box for another year. Stormy seems to be the most precious and valuable decoration Grandma owns. We have one on our tree back home just like it; Dad treats it with as much care as she does hers. Now that I think about it, our tree looks almost exactly like hers, and this is the first year I've noticed that too.

Stormy is a normal-looking reindeer, for a tree topper, I guess. He is about six inches tall and has bronze or goldish fur carved onto it. The fur seems to shimmer all the time, even when it is in the dark and not plugged in. It has a small antler rack with only three spikes on each side. It looks like it would be considered a young buck, possibly a yearling. His eyes are made of shiny black stones, polished so smooth that they look like they were made from some rare and precious gems. Stormy holds his head high as if he were alert and looking for something. His front legs are a little longer than the rear ones. The rear legs appear strong and powerful, giving him the look of grace and coordination. All this makes him look older and wiser than you would imagine a young buck would be. Around his neck is a collar with a nameplate. It's old and weathered leather and simply says "Stormy" in red scripted letters.

When he is plugged in and lit, the only thing that illuminates is the name "Stormy" in red, on the collar, but it seems to light up his whole body. Another thing I just noticed is the script that is used on this collar is the same used on the wooden box, the arrow-shaped sign, and the metal cocoa canister.

Dad is back on the stool now and has plugged Stormy into the cord that is used only for him. He climbs down and removes the stool from in front of the tree and places it next to Grandma's chair on her left side. Grandma hands him his cup of cocoa, and he sits down on the little stool. I am sitting closer to the tree on Dad's left side with my cocoa in my hand, which allows me to see the entire room including the tree, Grandma's face, and my dad sitting on that stool. He looks like a little child sitting there. His face seems to have changed somehow. He has a childlike grin, and his eyes are filled with anticipation. At this point, he looks like he could have been a five-year-old who was waiting for a big surprise. It was like he had never seen a Christmas tree before and couldn't wait for it to reveal its hidden secrets and special joys. Even though every year he sits in that same spot, this is the first time I remember looking at him and seeing him that way. It makes me wonder if he is like this every year or if something different is going on this year. No matter what it is, I'm still going to ask my questions.

Grandma was taking her last look at the tree before the lighting takes place. She is surveying each bulb, bell, and ornament, every branch from the bottom up. It is a seemingly slow process, but only takes about a minute.

She looks at the tinsel. I never understand why she spends so much time on the tinsel, but every year, it is the last thing that goes on the tree before Stormy, and it is put on one strand at a time. No one helps with this part of the tree trimming, just Grandma. It takes hours, not because it is so perfect but because there is *so* much of it. She uses boxes and boxes. There are literally hundreds, no, maybe thousands of strands of tinsel on her tree, each hung one at a time. The tinsel comes from more old packages. These packages open in the front and have a metal bar running across the middle, about an inch and a half from the top.

On New Year's Day, Grandma takes the tinsel off the tree the same way she puts it on, one strand at a time, and returns it to its boxes. It is the same tinsel every year in the same old packages that are older than me, older than my dad, and could be older than her too. The packages have the same script writing on the front with the same logo on it that says "The Great Northern Christmas Spirit & Tree Co."

I have never witnessed the process of taking down the Christmas tree because I always go to the movies on New Year's Day, every year for as long as I can remember. I see two and sometimes three movies; most of them are first-run movies I have been waiting to see for weeks or even months. I rarely go to the movies after the drive-in theaters close, until New Year's Day. Why don't I go before that? It's tradition, that's why. That's why I've never seen the tree being taken down. That is why I don't know where the tree goes, where it is replanted. I know it's not recycled or chopped up for firewood. I know it isn't put in a large white bag and hauled out to the curb for the garbage truck to pick up and take it to the dump with the empty boxes and colorful balled-up wrapping paper. I just don't know where the tree goes.

But I will this year because like I said, it's going to be one of those questions, one of the tough questions I ask. It's going to be one of those tough questions whose answer will give me the knowledge the adults keep from us so they can be wiser than us and keep us from being like them.

Chapter 4

Before I get any farther ahead of myself, you should know how the tree is decorated. It all starts with bringing the tree in and setting it up.

I know how they get the tree in the house and get it standing tall and straight. It is no special adult trick. My dad unties the tree from the SUV and slides it down the back to the ground. Then he goes in the garage and gets a hand truck and tilts the tree until the dolly can slide under the brown bag with all the roots and dirt. He ties it to the dolly and leans the dolly back and wheels it to the front porch. He pulls it up one step, then the next, and finally the third and final step to the top of the porch. This process is usually the only time that Dad uses words that don't really fit the Christmas theme. Then he rolls it into the house and wrestles it into a corner of the living room, the same corner every year, next to the front window where the TV usually sits. The TV has already been moved to a less prominent part of the room so it doesn't take any focus away from the tree.

When that is done and the tree is untied, Dad wheels the dolly back to the garage. At this point, the boxes containing all the decorations are brought in. There are just two boxes total, but they are pretty big. The first box has the tree skirt and lights and cords in it, and it also contains the manger scene with all its characters and a whole lot of miscellaneous decorations that Grandma displays throughout her house.

Dad wraps the tree skirt around the bag with the roots in it, and then we start decorating the tree. We always start with the lights. The first set of lights is pulled out and tested. We run a lead cord under the tree around back, and the first sets of lights are plugged into it. These lights are all white; there are several strands of one hundred lights each. Dad and I wrap them around the trunk from the bottom to the top, keeping them close to the trunk. The next sets of lights have small multicolored bulbs on them. We use a total of eight sets of the multicolored lights, and they are all one hundred lights per set too. We have to test each set to make sure there aren't any missing or burnt-out bulbs (which there always seems to be, even though I'm sure they are inspected before they are put away the year before), and we replace the bad bulbs.

After we are sure that every bulb from every set is in good working order, Dad and I begin the process of putting the bulbs on the tree. My dad starts at the bottom of the tree in the back and winds them around the branches counterclockwise, raising them one branch at a time until he reaches the top. He is very careful to keep them even all the way up, so all the gaps are filled. My job is to follow him around the tree and make sure that the strands don't get tangled. After six or seven trips around the tree, I get a little dizzy. The next and final sets of lights that are put on the tree are called the "blinker" bulbs. There are three sets of these. They are tested and hung in an up-and-down pattern, covering the tree in a zigzag.

With all the lights finally on the tree, Grandma takes several trips around the tree, inspecting it to make sure there are no gaps or dead spots. She always readjusts three or four areas, even though I can never see a difference when she is done.

We are done for now with the first box of decorations, and it is put aside till later. The next box is opened. This box contains all the ornaments, bells, and keepsakes. As with all Grandma's other decorations, they are all in their original packages and are in perfect condition.

With soft Christmas music playing in the background, Grandma starts handing out the ornaments. She gives me a small round shiny red one with the hook already attached. I know exactly what area of the tree it goes on because it is the same thing every year. I place it on the lowest branch near the back on the left-hand side of the tree. Grandma hands

The Legend of Stormy and the Great Northern Christmas Spirit & Tree Company

Dad one of the medium gold ones with its hook on it, and he works the other side of the tree, near the top. This goes on for an hour till all the ornaments are out of the box and on the tree in the right order and placement, as they are every year.

After the bulbs come the bells. Grandma has two types of bells. The first type looks like church bells, and the other type are jingle bells. These bells resemble the bells that you sometimes see horses wearing on Christmas cards when they are pulling sleighs filled with shiny packages through the snow past the church on what must be the perfect country Christmas morning; you know the ones I'm talking about.

I like the bells because I'm allowed to put them anywhere on the tree I choose, just so long as they are spaced evenly. Another thing I like about the bells is that this is usually when Dad concentrates on the cocoa and leaves me to work on the tree with just Grandma. After each bell has been placed and inspected, my portion of the decorating process is over. This is when Grandma hangs the specialty ornaments. These ornaments include everything from handmade bells with her kids' and grandkids' school pictures on them (there are two of these with my pictures on them) to fancy bulbs that had been gifts over the years.

Last, but certainly not least, comes the tinsel. As I said, Grandma does the tinsel. At this time, I usually leave the room. Normally, I go to the kitchen for a while and watch Dad slowly stir the pan of cocoa till I get bored with that, and with nothing left for me to do, I just wander the house, looking at the other decorations and pondering their place in Grandma's whole scheme of Christmas. It seems to me that each thing is placed precisely where it must be to somehow tell a story. She has her Christmas cards displayed on the ledge of the bay window in the kitchen in the order she has received them, with the first to arrive in the front and the latter ones in the back. There is mistletoe hanging over the entrance to the front door so she can steal a kiss from everyone who comes to visit and a slew of other Christmas-related things sprinkled about the rest of the house, including a complete Christmas village set above the cupboards in the kitchen, winding around in a semicircle. The village has stores and workshops. There are homes with decorated trees out front, and all around the little town are tiny figurines of people and even some reindeer-drawn sleighs. It is all quite odd and yet comforting at the same time. In the center of the village stand three decorated Christmas trees. The two on the outside are much shorter than the one in the center. This appears to be the focal point of the entire display.

I know the story the Christmas books tell. They have been read to me year after year. I know the story the holiday specials tell because I've seen every one of them with Dad at least ten times (he even knows all the words and songs, and he recites, sings, and performs them for me), each and every time they are on, and I know the story the Christmas songs tell too because these songs have filled my ears and mind and heart since before I was old enough to understand their words. All these things seem to play a huge part in the Christmas story that Dad and Grandma are somehow trying to tell me with their traditions.

This story is similar to the ones that everyone else's family tells, but in some way, ours is slightly different. Our story has a twist that I can't seem to grasp or understand, something that seems to be running in the background of the normal Christmas thing, like the music that plays in the background of a movie. You don't really hear the music unless you focus on it, but you know that without it, the movie would be incomplete, a story that I imagine has more to do with being an adult than anything else and is held as a close secret that gives them a power over me.

Well, this year, I've decided to hang around for the tinsel part. I figure this is when the adult thing happens, when the music is inserted into the movie, so to speak. This must be the time when the secrets are revealed and discussed, and I miss them because of my boredom. I can only assume this is when the answers I seek, the ones that usually have the replies of "Because," or "I said so," or "It's tradition" happen. Not this year. Not this time.

This time, I sit right there and watch as my grandma puts the tinsel on that tree. Grandma looks at me and smiles as she pulls out the boxes of tinsel with the fancy script on them that say "The Great Northern Christmas Spirit & Tree Co.," and with extreme care, she opens the first box and starts pulling the strands of tinsel out one by one and applying them to the branches of the tree. She continues this process over and over, hundreds, maybe thousands of times until every strand from every box is placed on the tree.

When she is done, the tree looks like one big icicle. Then she simply closes the tinsel boxes and carefully returns them to the box the decorations are stored in. That's it. No earth-shattering developments. No hidden secrets. No adult-type activities of any kind, just tinsel. At first, I felt like a fool, like, how paranoid could I be? But then I realized that this is part of the deception that adults use on us. This made me more determined than ever to ask the questions. This act of tinsel would not go without an explanation.

The time is now at hand. The tree is up. The decorations are all properly placed. The tinsel is complete, and Stormy, that ridiculous reindeer tree topper, is in place, waiting to be lit. Now is my time, my opportune moment. No one else is here yet. This is it; I'm not backing down (although I must admit I am excited and terrified at the same time). Here we go.

Grandma stands up, raises her cup of cocoa, and takes one last look at the tree, one last look at Stormy. She gives Dad the nod that signifies the tree is complete.

Normally, the rest of my family would be here at this time too, my aunts and uncles and all my cousins. My uncles would have helped with the tree and getting the decorations out. They would have put up the outside lights and manger scene in the yard and run all the power cords. They would have had the boys help them. My aunts would have had us girls helping them with the food and interior decorations. We would have spent the day baking and decorating cookies. We would have been making all types of snacks to enjoy the whole evening. There would have been shrimp with both melted butter and cocktail sauce. We would have made pizza bites. My aunts would make a cheese ball, and we girls would put out the crackers. We'd set out bowls of nuts and chips. There was always salsa and a melted spicy cheese dip too. The smell of all these foods also became part of that background music playing in the movies. All these things were the distractions the adults used on us so they could keep their secrets.

But everything was different this year. This year, it was just

Grandma, Dad, and me. My aunts and uncles were all delayed. They were all waiting out a freak winter storm that blew in. They all said they were on the way but would be delayed by as much as a day. There were a lot of discussions on the phone about what to do, and the final decision was for us to put up the tree and decorate it, and all the other traditions of food and decorating would happen when everyone else arrived. Nothing was normal this year. Everything was different; well, almost everything. Everything except that tree topper, of course. Stormy stayed the same.

As her tradition has always been, Grandma began to speak her final words before the tree lighting finally happens, the words that throughout the years I've come to believe actually usher in the wonderment of Christmas.

Grandma turns her gaze to me and says in a cheerful and joyous voice, "Now that the tree is complete, is there anyone who has anything they would like to ask me about Christmas?"

This is my time. This is what I have been waiting for. This is where I shall make my stand.

As I prepared to speak, to ask my questions, to prove I was ready to be part of the adult world, I was suddenly overcome with fear and panic. I almost spilled my cocoa. Beads of sweat ran down my forehead, and my throat became so dry that I was afraid I might not be able to breathe. Grandma looked right at me with a twinkle in her eye. It was as if she had been reading my mind these past few hours.

I turned from her gaze and looked at my dad sitting on that stool, and he too was looking at me. He still had that childlike look on his face and in his eyes. Now I was really freaking out. I took as deep a breath as I could, sipped on my cocoa, and with all the adult confidence I could muster, looked directly at both of them and squeaked out, "All of my friends have a star or an angel or even a red bow at the top of their trees. Even the trees at the mall and the ones in the Christmas shows usually have a star. Why do you have a stupid reindeer named Stormy on the top of your tree?"

The room seemed to go dark all around me. It was as if all the light was being sucked out. At the same time, I started to lose my hearing

The Legend of Stormy and the Great Northern Christmas Spirit & Tree Company

too. Maybe I was fainting or even dying. Grandma and Dad's faces were fading, and though it looked like they were trying to talk to me, I couldn't hear their voices. It was like I was on an airplane climbing into the sky, and my ears were plugging up, and I couldn't swallow and clear them up. The room continued to grow darker, and now all I could see were their outlines. I was sure I was blacking out because now all I could see was the reindeer at the top of the tree, the reindeer with the shimmering bronze, goldish fur. The stupid reindeer with the leather collar on it, the collar with the fancy red script that simply says "Stormy," and the collar appears to be lighting up the entire room with a warm red glow, even though it hasn't even been plugged in yet. The warmth of that glow is now filling every expanse of space in the room, but not only in this room but in the entire house.

I almost felt it might even be filling me with a sort of magic power I couldn't fight off, even if I wanted to. It was as if that warm glow was filling the very essence of space and time. I don't know how, but for a brief moment, it was almost as if Stormy had come to life. At one point, I even thought that I heard Christmas carols, filling what was left of my quickly fading grip on reality.

I have heard that as you are about to die, your life flashes before your eyes. Is this what I was experiencing? What else could it be? All I could see in this warm red glow were quick scenes from my past, scenes I had almost forgotten, Christmas scenes, which were from a long time ago. I could see the snow outside the living room window of the little house we lived in when I was two or three. I saw the Christmas lights from the houses across the street glittering and dancing off of the snow. The reflection of those lights in the snow seemed to magnify their beauty a million times over.

I suddenly saw the fireplace Dad made for me out of cardboard and paint when I was five. He made it because I told him I was worried Santa wouldn't be able to deliver any presents to me because our house didn't have a chimney. I remembered he even let me paint the cardboard logs and fire he had put in it. I painted the logs light brown with some crooked black lines running through them to make it look like bark. The flames were red on the lower part with yellow tips to make it look like they were really burning. For a more authentic look, Dad added a cheap flickering electric light behind the fake flames so it appeared as if the logs were really on fire.

I could even remember sitting in front of it, believing I could feel heat coming off the fake logs with the fake flames illuminated with the flickering light bulb causing a dull glow on the stockings we had hung on the front of it, the stockings that had our names written on them in glitter. These were the stockings my dad had let me sprinkle glitter over the glue we used to write our names in the fluffy white area at the top.

After that, I remembered another scene from my past, a scene that changed everything Christmas for me, forever. It was a scene where I came home from school the day of Christmas break in fifth grade and waited by the fireplace made from cardboard with the fake flames I had painted and the cheap light to make it appear to be real, and I could no longer feel the heat. I remember standing next to that fireplace with my glitter-covered stocking in my hand, most of the glitter gone, and just waiting for Dad to come home.

I remember the look on his face as he entered the room and asked what was wrong. I can still see his expression when I announced that Santa was a fake. Even though I understood and believed in the reason we celebrate Christmas, the whole Santa, flying reindeer, toy-making elves, and North Pole thing was over for me. At my Christmas party earlier in the day at school, I overheard a couple of the other kids' parents. They were talking about how long they thought they could keep up this story, before their kids found out the truth. It was then I overheard my friend Jo Ellen's mom say that Jo Ellen had figured it out last year, but she promised not to tell anyone.

Those were the last flashbacks from my life I had, and I was sure it was over. Right then, I started to see some brightness. Some light was making its way into my mind and maybe my eyes. I started to hear sounds. The sounds were faint and muffled at first but became louder and clearer. I was making out shapes in the distance, and they came from the same direction as the sounds I was hearing. Clearer and clearer, louder and louder, till all at once, I was back.

"Brandi, are you okay? Brandi, can you hear us? Are you all right?"

It was Dad and Grandma. They were sitting there just as they had been before everything went dark. They looked at me with a touch of worry, but not fear. Then Grandma looked at my dad, and he gave her what appeared to be a nod of approval, and she said, "Well, I guess it's time you heard the truth."

Chapter 5

"I know this going to be hard to believe," Grandma began, "but if you hear me out, I think you will understand. If you want to know about Stormy the reindeer, and why I have him as the tree topper on my Christmas tree, then I suggest you get comfortable and take a deep sip of your cocoa because it's not only Stormy you need to know about, it has to do with the tree, the decorations, the cocoa, and the traditions: the whole thing. When it comes right down to it, it has to do with something even bigger than all of that. It has to do with the spirit of Christmas itself, that deep-down innocence and joy, which can only be understood in the wide eyes of a child on Christmas Eve. This type of joy can only be seen in the eyes of children, children full of the anticipation for things they have never witnessed and yet believe in with their whole heart, soul, and mind. This is the kind of spirit that changes people forever. It changes them so completely that they cannot help but have an effect on the people around them, without even knowing it. Are you sure you are ready for this? Are you ready to hear this story, Brandi? Are you prepared to accept the responsibility that comes with this powerful knowledge?"

I'd be lying if I said I wasn't a little afraid at this point. The truth is, I was never so terrified in my life. But if I wanted to be treated like an adult, then I would have to act like one (or at least what I thought one acted like), and sit there and listen to this hidden truth.

I looked at Dad; he still had that same childlike look on his face, the one I had seen when he sat down on the stool next to Grandma. I knew at that point, he wasn't going to help me decide, but he wasn't going to stop me, either. It was almost like he had been waiting for me to ask all along, like he had been waiting for this day all of my life. He appeared to be anticipating this day as much as I was. That scared me almost more than challenging the tradition of the Stormy tree topper itself. That's when I looked up at Grandma and uttered a single word, the word that I was sure would change my life forever. A single word, as it turns out, that would separate me from my childhood past and catapult me into the world of the adults. It was just a simple word, three letters, one syllable, a common word that, when spoken out loud, had the potential to alter my place in this world forever.

I took a deep drink of my cocoa, looked past the gaze of my dad, and with all my strength looked straight into Grandma's eyes and uttered that life-altering three-letter word: Yes. I said yes, meaning I was ready. I was ready to be changed. I was ready for the truth. I was ready to join that elite group of people known as adults.

Grandma sat back down slowly. She shut her eyes and took a long, slow sip of her cocoa. Dad turned and looked at her, and after what seemed like an eternity, she opened her eyes. She looked at my dad and then at me, and it was as if she had been transported to a different place or even a different time altogether. Her eyes were different. They appeared to be holding an ancient secret that was bursting to be released, something that only a few living people could understand and even fewer had ever experienced. Her eyes seemed to belong to someone else altogether. They appeared to have changed, just like Dad's had. They had the look of pure joy and innocence. It was then that she began her story.

"Brandi," she began, "I was about your age when I started to question the whole Christmas thing. I wondered why so much effort was put into creating the perfect Christmas season, why my parents, my grandparents, and all my neighbors worked so hard to prepare for a single day. Why was it that at this time in December, in the middle of the winter, people from all walks of life turned from their normal routines and put so much effort into a single project? Schools would decorate their halls and classrooms with those colorful chains the students made with construction paper and glue sticks. The bands and choirs put on holiday concerts, and the whole community would turn out just to hear the children sing silly songs about Old St. Nick or jingling sleigh bells. Stores put up special displays and sold foods and candies and toys that were not available at any other time of the year.

"All of a sudden, everyone wanted to see snow everywhere, when the rest of the time, it seemed like snow was a huge inconvenience. All these things happened for no logical or rational reason.

"I started talking with my friends about all these things. Some of them were afraid to even discuss it, like they were going to put a curse on themselves or something. Some had no opinion at all. But some of the others, the ones who always wanted to be in control of everything, had very strong opinions. They banded together and denounced the whole thing as just a way for their parents and other adults to keep them from knowing the truth.

"They said this thing called Christmas was just made up so that children would behave as they wanted them to. It was just a way to control all of us without having to explain why we should act as they say we should. It was just another technique to keep us from becoming adults, a way of molding us to fit the model of behavior they wanted. The whole Santa and his reindeer thing is a ploy to control us, and what is up with the toy-making elves? Last but not least, the naughty and nice list, which is again just another tool of manipulation. If you add all these things up and include in the idea of being rewarded with gifts on Christmas morning for our good behavior, it's just another adult control thing. That's what we decided.

"That is when I, just like you, Brandi, decided that I would be fooled no more. I decided that even though I really liked all the things that the Christmas season brought, the presents and decorations, the food and candies, the silly songs and TV specials, all the well wishes and good cheer, I would no longer be controlled by these things. I decided I would do as I thought fit. I would act like I wanted because it wouldn't really change anything, and I guess I was right.

"The holidays went by as they always did. The tree and the house were decorated. We watched the Christmas shows and specials. We shopped and wrapped presents (although beginning with that year, my presents seemed a bit more practical and a lot less fun). We sang carols and gathered together for meals and wishes of good cheer. Christmas cards were sent and received. Yep, even though I chose to give up the whole North Pole, Santa, elves, and reindeer thing, Christmas came and went just like it always did, and nobody seemed to notice any difference in me at all. We had a party on New Year's Eve. We watched football New Year's Day. We ate and drank the same foods and drinks that we would have anyway. Nothing changed.

"Then it was all over. The tree and decorations came down and were put away. The candies were gone. The presents were all open and being used as if they had always been here. Life returned to normal. It was back to school and work for everyone, and the joy and anticipation just seemed to slip away and was replaced by daily life. That's pretty much how it went for the next several years.

"As the years went by and I got older, I also grew farther and farther away from the Christmas of my youth, and I participated less in the traditions of my family. As the years passed, I somehow lost the magic and wonder that came with Christmas and decided that it was all just a reason for the world to step back and regroup and a way to regain its collective sanity. It was just a way for everyone to bond together for a brief time every year so that they could find a reason to make it through all that life puts on them. That is what I had come to believe. And I figured the end of December was as good a time as any for this reset to happen, right in the middle of winter, when most of the world was dealing with fewer hours of daylight and colder temperatures. Right when people seemed to need a reason to hope that life was going to get better and easier.

"The older I got, the more I looked at it this way. The more I looked at it this way, the less I seemed to care about the whole thing, and the less I cared about the whole thing, the less I participated in its traditions. This just continued till I didn't really do Christmas at all.

"When I was twenty-two, I decided I had more important things to do than waste three or four weeks of my life preparing for and participating in the Christmas thing. No presents, no cookies, no carols, no TV specials, no hot cocoa, no family, no warm wishes to strangers, no cards, no decorations, not even a tree. For the first time in my life, I felt like an adult. I felt that I had finally broken the bonds of childhood and taken control of my life. It was me against the world, and I had this. Because I had taken this control, it provided me with what would turn out to be the chance of a lifetime, a chance to prove to the world and to everyone who knew me just how strong and grown up I was."

Chapter 6

"The year was 1971," Grandma continued, "and I was just six months out of college. After the four grueling years of study and preparation, the tests and the papers and all the sleepless nights of cramming for exams, my time for learning had ended. I was one step closer to my lifelong dream of controlling my own destiny.

"All through middle school and high school, I dreamed of a life in the world of broadcasting. I was on the school paper in eighth grade and joined the video club in high school. It was this club that showed me what I wanted to do for the rest of my life. This small video club changed my dreams and desires forever. It was during my time in this club I decided what path I would choose for my future.

"The video club started out as just a group of students from all four grades who didn't really fit in anywhere else in the high school scene. High school had four distinct areas of separation, well, at least in my school and in my time. The first and most prestigious group were the athletes. The athletes were in control of the school. Not just the halls and the classrooms but the entire school. They controlled the teachers, the administrators, and even the community itself. This group was made up of students from the other three areas, but while they were participating in their chosen specialties, whether it was football, the sport that seemed to have the most power, basketball, track, or volleyball, which back in those days was the only sport that girls could participate in, the athletes always enjoyed the power and benefits of assumed physical prowess.

"The next group in line, who also seemed to have a certain amount of power, were the scholars. The scholars were not as popular as the athletes, although many of the scholars were also athletes and enjoyed almost unlimited freedom because of this dual status; the rest of the scholars still enjoyed a good deal of power and freedom due to the simple fact they could understand and retain a lot of useless information and then transfer that information on to a paper the teachers would pass out on Fridays in each class, papers the teachers called tests.

"The last two groups of students, the general population and the bad kids, shared the rest of school life. These students held about the same status in school life. I know this because these were the groups my entire school career was played out in. Sometimes I was just a general population student, and sometimes I was regarded as a bad kid. This was not because I was either one, but it was because I didn't belong in the first two groups; that's all. Being in the last two groups was neither good nor bad; it was just what it was. When you are stuck with this status in high school, you had to find some way to belong, a place to make your mark, so to speak.

"Some of us chose to just exist, just make it through and get past high school and start our lives, and that was fine. The rest of us, and this included me, tried to make our mark by joining various clubs. We had band and choir, chess club, library student staff, teachers' aides, and video club. I chose video club because it seemed to be the least challenging club and still had fun-looking projects to do. In video club, we were assigned to record all the sporting events for the coaches, so we got to go to them for free and had access to the entire venues. We had cool passes we would hang around our necks on lanyards, like they were ribbons we had won. Even though no one really cared much about us, we still enjoyed a little power and freedom, and it was good enough for me.

"It was in my sophomore year, my second year in video club, when the change occurred, the change that set me on my quest and gave me my focus for college and my future. It was in that year a new teacher arrived at our school, a teacher who was unlike any teacher I had ever known before and would ever experience again."

* * *

As Grandma's story continued, I wondered if she was just trying to buy time. Although it was kind of interesting and gave me a look into her past and what made her the person she was today, I just couldn't see how this was going to help me understand the whole Stormy the reindeer thing. It just didn't seem to be leading to the answers about these Christmas traditions I sought. But it was something to pass the time as the snow continued to fall outside and we waited for the rest of the family to arrive. So I took another sip of my cocoa and listened on.

* * *

Grandma continued, "The teacher's name was Miss Penny. Now, Miss Penny was not only new to our school, but she was new to teaching altogether. She was just one year out of college; this was her first full-time position. She was brought in to teach what they called an elective. An elective was a class students could take instead of study hall. It gave us credits that counted toward graduation but weren't regular curriculum like math or history or language arts. It was also a well-known fact you could get a good grade with little or no homework in an elective, and those grades would raise your average, so many students chose to take elective courses, and I was one of them.

"The class Miss Penny taught was called mythology and folklore and dealt with things such as the Greek gods and fairy tales and all such matters."

* * *

Now was when I thought Grandma was going to reveal her change of heart about the whole Santa thing. This teacher, Miss Penny, must have taught about the myth of the North Pole, flying reindeers, and toy-making elves during this class. She would tell me how she had the truth revealed to her by this young teacher just out of college. She continued.

* * *

"I took Miss Penny's class in the first semester, right from the beginning of the year. She taught from the heart as much as from the book. She talked to the students more like adults than kids. I liked that a lot.

"Just before the second football game of the season, my life was changed again. Mr. Everett, the advisor to the video club, my video club, announced he was stepping down from the position because he had taken a promotion and would not have time to be our advisor. We were stunned. We all looked at each other and then at Mr. Everett. Kenny B was the first to speak. Kenny B was a senior and the president of the video club and was pretty popular around school, so he gave the club a good reputation and some minor respect. Kenny B said what was on all of our minds. He asked, 'What will happen to the video club?'

"Mr. Everett stood up and looked at each of us, one at a time, his face void of all emotion, nothing that gave us hope for the future of our club. Then his eyes lit up a little. He smiled and said, 'I would like to thank you all for the time we have had together as a group. You have taught me a great deal these past years. The things that you have accomplished in this time have helped me to grow as a teacher, an advisor, and a person. Each one of you should be proud of yourselves. It is the experience I gained from you that has given me the confidence to further my career and take the position at the district. I will miss each and every one of you, but I will take the things we learned and did here in our group with me each and every day of my life.'

"I looked around me, and all I saw was sadness. Even Kenny appeared to have tears welling up in his eyes. I thought I was about to cry myself. What would we do? We loved our club. We loved the lanyards and the passes they held, like ribbons we had won. We loved the power we felt when they let us in the games for free and the access we were given. What would we do now? How would we fit in after this? Before we all broke down in despair, in walked Miss Penny. She walked right up to Mr. Everett, and he turned to us and said, 'Some of you may already know Miss Penny.' A few of us from her class gave her a weak wave. 'Miss Penny has graciously agreed to take my place as video club advisor. I hope you will give her the same respect and joy you have given me. I know as a group you will continue to challenge yourselves and make us all proud. Again I thank you.' He walked around and shook each of our hands and left.

"Miss Penny took over right then and there. It was as if she had been doing this all her life.

"The video footage of that Friday's game was the best it had ever been. Miss Penny had showed us all about angles and lighting and focus, and we were able to apply those lessons at the game.

"At our next meeting the following Monday, she told us she had studied theater and media in college. She said her college major was in teaching but her minor and her passion was to produce television news; there wasn't a big demand for female news producers in those days, but she said the times were changing. She said she took the job at our school because of the chance to one day be the advisor of the video club. She said this club was going to set the standard for high school video clubs across the country. She already had a plan to expand our role in the school. We would still be doing the games and enjoying our access and privileges, but if everyone worked together as a team, we could create our own high school news crew, complete with anchors, reporters, producers, directors, and camera personnel.

"She was right. We started right after football season and before basketball. The first year, we looked really rough, but we got better. I started out behind the camera and then went on to be a reporter. By the time my senior year came around, I was club president and the news director. Our news program became a pilot program for other schools, and because of its success, we got to travel around to other schools and help them start up their video clubs.

"We were no longer just the general population students; we created a class of our own, a class anyone from any group in the school, athletes, scholars, and all the rest, could find a place to fit in and be proud. This was when I decided what I wanted to do the rest of my life. I wanted to work in the media. I wanted to work in the news. I wanted to direct and produce the news on TV."

Chapter 7

"I went off to college in the fall," Grandma continued, "and studied hard, and that was the first year that Christmas almost slipped by me. I made it home the day before Christmas Eve and did some quick shopping and wrapping, but the rest of the stuff was already done.

"The outside lights were up. The house was decorated, and the baking was done. Even the tree was done. The one thing I do remember that year was the smell of the tree when I first entered the house. I remember commenting on how much it smelled like Christmas in the house. Something about the smell of the evergreen tree just made it feel like Christmas. Maybe it was just all the years with a live tree and its sweet and distinct smell filling the house at this time of the year that triggered these feelings and memories. Whatever it was, it was as close to my childhood memories of Christmas as I was going to get.

"I went back to school before the New Year so I could get a jump on the next semester. The next two years were much the same. Then in my senior year of college, I didn't come home for Christmas at all. I did some special projects for different local news stations, intern stuff, and just stayed in my dorm on Christmas Eve and Christmas Day. I did buy a small artificial tree I found at the local thrift store near campus, but I was so caught up in my own life and desires, I even forgot to plug it in and light it up."

* * *

At this point, I found myself feeling sorry for Grandma. I couldn't believe that this woman who had so many traditions and spent so much time on Christmas had almost let Christmas slip completely by. It's hard for me to believe she could have ever let even one Christmas pass her by. Now I was really interested in where this story was going. What could have happened to bring back her Christmas spirit? What could make someone who had almost given Christmas up completely embrace the season with all the joy and love of a child? She even passed those feelings and emotions on to the rest of her family. Now more than ever, I wanted to know. She must have sensed what I was feeling because she looked at me a little more intensely and continued.

* * *

"I ended up graduating near the top of my class and was given a job at WXMAS TV 5. They liked the work I had done while I was an intern for them. This was amazing because women were just starting to be taken seriously in TV, and I was one of the few who were given the chance to prove myself.

"This was the best time in my life. I was focused and willing to learn anything. I started as an assistant to the camera department, which meant I worked with the various video crews. Most of the time, I would just assign equipment to the crews for remote broadcasts and then check the equipment back in and make sure everything was ready and in good working order for the next remote shoot. I also set up and maintained the newsroom cameras.

"This was exciting for me because I was able to be all around the studio and had access to all parts of the process, including editing and the control room, where all the magic was made. I even had a lanyard with a badge on it. The badge had my name and picture on it, just like the one I had in high school, which had given me full access to the football and basketball games.

"I was loving life. I had a few opportunities to film some of the remote broadcasts, and it turned out those hints Miss Penny had given us back in high school worked in the real world too.

"By the time Halloween arrived, I was doing more remote video shoots than anything else and was being considered for a full-time position as camerawoman. All was just as I had dreamed. The work was demanding, and the hours were long and always changing because news happens when news happens.

"Thanksgiving came, and I went home. I was only home for Thanksgiving Day and back to work on Friday. The station was getting ready to do some Christmas promos and remotes. This is the time of year when many of the crew schedule their vacations and time off to be with their families over the holiday. I thought about putting in for December 21 through 26 and traveling back home to be with my family too because I was feeling guilty about not participating in the family holiday traditions the past few years.

"Just before I filed for the time off, John, the news director, called me into his office. I was a little worried about what he might want. This is also the time of the year when two things happen in the TV news business. First, and of course the best, is this is when the promotions are handed out, and with them sometimes a modest bonus check (one that I could really use). The other thing that happens this time of year is the layoffs. I know this seems cruel, especially just before Christmas, but the budget for the next year has to be met. As they say, it's not personal; it's just business. Say it anyway you want to, it still sucks.

"John was a fair man when it came to business. He treated everyone equally. He was only in his forties, but the demands of the job left him with gray hair, and the reading glasses he always wore near the edge of his nose made him look like he was nearer to his late fifties. I sat outside his office on the edge of my chair, with Susan, the office receptionist, whom everyone always commented actually ran the station. I tried to calm myself. I thought of every argument I could to save my job and practiced them in my head.

"John opened his door and motioned for me to come in. I took a quick look over at Susan, and she gave me a reassuring smile. I stood up, walked into the office, and closed the door behind me.

"I had talked to John many times before this day, and he always had a stern kindness about him. I knew he always came right to the point because if you're in the news business, you have to get things done fast and done right the first time. He sat down behind a pile of papers on his desk and told me to have a seat.

"I couldn't tell from his tone which way this meeting was going to go, but I just couldn't see it going my way; a bonus check was doubtful, a promotion equally as doubtful. At this point, I figured the best I could hope for was a 'Thank you and keep up the good work.'

"As I anticipated, he got right to the point: 'Jane,' he said, 'I know it's nearing Christmas and all.'

"My heart sank, and I could feel tears well in my eyes, but I fought them back and sat up straight. He continued, and at first, I couldn't hear him or even see him clearly, but then as I slowly regained my composure, all I heard was 'Think about it and get back to me as soon as you can.'

"I blinked a few times and said, 'I'm sorry, I didn't quite get all that.' He looked at me and started over.

"'I know it's short notice,' he began again, 'but I was hoping if you didn't have any plans for the week before Christmas, you would consider doing a special piece on the yearly migration of reindeer in Alaska. This would be all you: the photography, the editing, the writing, even the on-air reporting. It's a big sacrifice, but I think you would be great for the job.'

"I almost passed out right then and there. I couldn't believe it. This is everything that I hoped, no, dreamed about, ever since my sophomore year in high school. Without even considering what it might entail, I stood up and said, 'Yes, yes, I'll do it.'

"He stood up, smiled, shook my hand, and said, 'Well, you better get started then; you leave soon. Susan will set you up with an account and prepare your agenda. See her on Monday for the final details. Enjoy this and make us all proud.'

"With that, I just nodded my head, turned, and walked out. By the stare I got from Susan as I exited John's office, I must have been smiling like a crazy person, but I didn't care."

Chapter 8

"I went right to work on my new assignment," Grandma went on. "I headed straight to the library and checked out several books on reindeer, which are actually called caribou in Alaska. Some of the books were about the migration, some were picture books, and one was about the myth of flying reindeer (one was a children's book about Santa and his flying reindeer), but research is research, and I wanted to cover all my bases.

"I also picked out books that dealt with different aspects of life in Alaska: the weather, the customs, the people, and the landscapes. I studied this vast array of information and used it to set my travel plans, decide my wardrobe, and choose my equipment and supplies. I had to propose a budget for the trip, and I wanted to prove I could be professional and efficient. I began the long and complicated process of planning this extreme remote shoot.

"The first thing I learned was the reindeer migration happened in a narrow window of time in Alaska. I would only have about two days to catch it, and the lighting would only be available for about three hours each of those days, and that didn't take into account the weather, which could disrupt the migration and the filming process and even my travel plans for this trip. Another thing I learned is the migration takes place in a remote area of the state that offered excellent backgrounds, full of evergreen forests and snow-peaked mountains. With all the things I learned in college and the stuff Miss Penny taught me about angles and lighting, plus my experience working remotes at WXMAS, I was confident I would get some spectacular footage. Through the magic of editing, my final piece would be shown in multiple air slots throughout the news day, maybe even the evening newscast, the most watched time of the day. This could make my career or break it, if anything went wrong, and this far from home, in this remote area, with no backup, anything could go wrong."

* * *

Grandma was really into this story. She was in a different state of mind or maybe a different world altogether. I looked into her eyes as she told her story, and they looked younger. They had acquired a sparkle I couldn't quite grasp, a gleam that gave me a feeling of safety and hope. I didn't understand it, but I felt it, nonetheless. I looked over at my dad briefly, and he seemed mesmerized by her story, even though I was sure he had heard it before. The whole world seemed to stop and disappear while she spoke. I took another sip of my cocoa and settled back for more.

* * *

Grandma continued, "The more I studied and planned, the more I worried I might have gotten myself in too deep with this assignment. The trip alone was very daunting. Alaska is a very long way from Indiana, where I was living at the time. I would have to drive to Detroit and catch a flight to Minneapolis. From Minneapolis, I would fly to Anchorage and finally end up in Fairbanks, Alaska. All told, the flights themselves could take ten hours in the air. Then who knew how long it would be to get to the migration itself. I was really starting to worry myself, but I kept at it.

"After two days of studying and preparing, I finally took action. I went to a military surplus store and bought my Alaska winter gear. I started with a cap. I had seen where the locals wore these fur-lined caps with ear flaps attached; when they were down and snapped under the chin, they would cover most of the sides of your face. When the flaps were up, the hat just made you look like some crazy pilot who should be crop-dusting the fields of Kansas or something.

"The next thing I picked was an insulated face mask with a triangle nose cover. This mask made me look like I had a scarecrow's face when I tried it on. The mask also had an opening for the mouth with small holes in it for breathing. It was smooth and shiny on the outside and had an itchy felt lining on the inside. The adjustable straps that held it on my face snapped to the cheek area and went around behind the head.

"Next, I had to get a good warm coat. The coats I had seen in the library books were called parkas. I approached an older gentleman who was stocking hunting vests on a rack next to a display of camping gear and asked him where I could find such a coat. He was a rugged outdoor type with balding grayish hair and a warm smile. He introduced himself as Terry. Terry mentioned to me that he and his wife, Kathy, owned the store and said he would be happy to help me out. He asked me if I was specifically looking for parkas or just a good warm coat, so I explained the whole trip to Alaska to cover the reindeer migration.

He took me to the back of the store and showed me three racks of parkas. Some were camouflage, some were navy blue, and there were some all-white ones with white fur trim around the hood, sleeves, and around the bottom. I tried on several of the white ones and picked one that came down to my midthigh. Terry said I made a great choice. He said the one I had picked had several pockets on the inside, and the outside had two deep zippered pockets I could keep my gloves and other necessities in. This worked out perfect because I knew I would need a place to carry a spare lens and at least one extra battery for my video camera; I thought I looked good in this coat, and if I was going to do a remote shoot for the news, I wanted to look as good as possible.

"After picking out my coat, Terry took me to the section of the store with the gloves and talked me into a pair of light ones with this new material lining the inside that was very thin, but he said it would keep me warm to 10 degrees below zero, and I would still be able to use my hands and fingers as if I didn't have any gloves on at all. I also picked out an oversized pair of mittens to wear over the gloves and keep my hands toasty warm, no matter how cold it got outside.

"I believed I had everything I needed, but Terry, being a true salesman, asked if I had any insulated underwear or snow pants. He also asked if I had boots. I bought two pairs of insulated long johns, a pair of white shiny ski pants to match my parka, and six pairs of socks made with the same thin material as my gloves. Last but not least, I bought a pair of snow boots. These boots were different from any other boots I had ever seen. They were white rubber, and even though I only needed a ladies size 7½, they looked like a men's size 10. They had thick soles to protect me from the snow and ice, with a tread on the bottom. The tread looked like the snow tires Dad put on his truck just before the first snowfall of the winter. What really caught my attention were the air valves protruding from the outside of each boot.

Terry explained to me the air valves were just like the ones I have on my car tires. The valves were used to fill the boots with air after you put them on. This helped to fit them to your feet, and the air acted as a natural insulator from the cold. He assured me these boots, once filled with air, would keep my feet completely warm and dry, even in temperatures of 50 degrees below zero. And then he sold me a mini air pump so I could pump them up anywhere (like I said, he was a really good salesman). We couldn't think of anything I missed, so I went to the counter to check out.

"Ahead of me at the checkout counter was a man with a scruffy beard wearing the same type of hat I was just about to buy. He purchased some ice fishing gear and a fancy knife. I put all my subzero gear on the counter, and a woman ('Kathy' was on her name tag, so I figured she was Terry's wife) greeted me with a smile and a pleasant "Hello" and began ringing me out. She looked at the stuff I had put on the counter and then looked up at me. With a big grin and a sarcastic tone, she asked, 'What are you planning on doing, going to the North Pole or something?'

"I remember looking straight at her with a huge smile on my face and simply replying, 'Yes, yes, I am.'

"She laughed a hearty laugh, took my money, and wished me a safe trip, and I was on my way."

* * *

At this point, I was still wondering if Grandma was ever going to get to the point. She still seemed to be just wasting time until the rest of the family could arrive. The snow outside was letting up a little, and we still hadn't lit up Stormy yet. I took another sip of my cocoa, and she continued.

* * *

"From the surplus store, I went across town to the travel agency WXMAS uses for all its travel needs. I had an appointment with a woman named Crystal. Susan, the station's secretary, had arranged it all for me. Crystal was just finishing up with an older couple. They were booking some sort of cruise and were asking a whole bunch of questions. Crystal finished up with the older couple and walked them to the door. She shook their hands, smiled, and wished them a good day. She thanked them for coming in, turned to me, smiled, and apologized for keeping me waiting.

"I liked her instantly. She was a petite young woman. Her smile was real and not just for show. Her face showed compassion, and her eyes were honest. She walked up to me, shook my hand, and said, 'You must be Jane. Please have a seat. I will be with you in a quick minute.'

"Crystal took the older couple's papers to a woman behind the counter near the back of the store and spoke with her for a few minutes. While I waited, I looked around. I noticed all the posters strategically placed around the lobby and on the walls. Most of them were of places like southern Florida and California or exotic islands like Aruba, Jamaica, and the Bahamas. All of them had beaches and palm trees and deep blue water lapping the shore. It made sense to me because in Indiana in the middle of December, people were looking for an escape from the cold and snow, and that is certainly what they were selling here. There were also a few posters of ski trips to places in Colorado and Utah and upstate New York, but mostly just palm trees and beaches and the blue water.

"Crystal returned and sat down at her desk across from me, and as she apologized again for keeping me waiting, I couldn't help but notice she had a perfect tan. It was as if she had just come from one of those beaches with the blue water and palm trees, and maybe she did. Her hair was cropped short and kind of hung down across her left eye, which gave her a European look, but her Indiana accent said she was a hometown Midwestern girl.

"She told me Susan had phoned ahead and told her I was planning a business trip a bit north and west of Indiana. We both laughed, and she pulled out a folder with my name on it. She said according to the information she was given, I was headed to the North Pole. I said that was sort of right, but I was really just heading to Alaska to film the reindeer migration and would need to get to Fairbanks. She smiled and told me that, for sure I was going to Fairbanks, but my ultimate destination was North Pole: North Pole, Alaska that is. Before I could correct her, she pulled out a map of Alaska and pointed to a small dot near Fairbanks. This small dot was called North Pole, and for sure it was in Alaska, about one hundred miles south of the Arctic Circle. She even said there was a place called Santa's Castle in North Pole.

* * *

Now Grandma's story was taking shape. North Pole Alaska, Santa's Castle, reindeer. What else could there be? All I need now is how Stormy fits in to the whole thing.

* * *

Grandma said she asked Crystal if she had ever been to Alaska, and she explained that she went there last year, but in the summer. Almost no one goes there in the winter. The cold is brutal at this time of the year. It snows almost every day, and the temperature can go as low as 50 below zero. I was glad I bought the boots, the mittens, and the long johns.

"Crystal had already done all the research for the travel plans. She showed me my itinerary, which took me out of Detroit Metro Airport to Minneapolis. I was to change planes in Minneapolis and then fly to Anchorage. Once again, I would change planes and end up in

Fairbanks. The trip from Detroit to Minneapolis was two hours. There was a two-hour layover, and then the flight to Anchorage was six hours. The trip from Anchorage to Fairbanks was another hour. It sounded like a long day to me, but what could I do?

"Crystal told me that once I got to Fairbanks, my guide would take over. She said his name was Earl, and he was from the Great Northern Christmas Spirit & Tree Co. He would take care of me until my return trip to Detroit."

* * *

Bang. Now we were getting somewhere; finally, a connection to the whole traditions thing. Now the real story would begin. I was thinking that I was going to need some more cocoa, and Dad must have sensed it because as I drained the last drops from my cup, he had the pan with the sweet hot cocoa and eight miniature marshmallows ready to refill me, even before I asked. He filled Grandma's and his own at the same time. After a deep sip of her freshly refilled cocoa, Grandma took a breath and continued on.

* * *

"I signed several papers," she said, "and took the color brochures Crystal had assembled for me. She went over the dates and times again, and then she asked if I had any other questions. I told her no, and we both stood up. Crystal escorted me to the door and took my hands and pulled me close. She gave me a little hug, the kind of hug family members give each other when they say goodbye, and whispered in my ear, 'Good luck and have fun, but be safe; don't take any unnecessary risks.'

"As I left the travel agency, I had an odd feeling Crystal knew something about this trip she wasn't telling me. I thought about it for a moment but just shook it off and headed back to my apartment to set my final preparations."

Chapter 9

Grandma continued, "I got back to my apartment just after two in the afternoon and unloaded all the stuff I had acquired that day. I started with the white rubber snow boots, the ones with the air valves sticking out the sides. I set them at the foot of my bed, along with the mini air pump. Alongside the boots, I laid out the socks and then put the long johns on the end of the bed, with the legs hanging over and settling on the boots. I laid the white fur-lined parka on top of the long johns, with the bottom of the coat covering the waist of the long johns. I set the gloves and mittens at the ends of the sleeves of the parka, and then I put the mask and cap inside the parka's hood. I wish I had taken a picture of it as it lay there; it would have made a humorous addition to the piece I was about to undertake.

"I stared at my newly acquired North Pole ware and I thought to myself, *This must be what astronauts feel like the night before a trip to the moon*, and it might as well have been the moon I was going to. Up to this point in my life, the farthest I had ever traveled from home was a camping trip to Kentucky with my uncle and cousins when I was about eleven years old, and we drove there.

"The phone rang, bringing me back to reality. I answered, and it was John. He wanted to make sure I wasn't backing out, and I assured him I wasn't. He told me to take the next couple of days off and prepare for my adventure, and I thanked him.

"I decided to go to the TV station anyway and was greeted by Scott, the security guard. He welcomed me with his ever-present smile.

His smile always gave me a feeling of security and reassurance. Before working at the station, Scott had been a policeman for the city, and after retiring, he missed helping people, so he took the job as head of security here at the TV station. Scott had a dry, sarcastic sense of humor and seemed to blend in the background, but when he was there, you always knew, no matter what was happening, everything was going to be all right.

"I went right to the newsroom, and things were moving along as normal. Mike, the stage manager, was going over the details of today's broadcast with the camera crew. He was giving instructions to Linda and Susie, (not to be confused with Susan the receptionist), normally I worked the morning crew but Linda was filling in for me as I prepared for my trip. Susie was busy checking the news copy and prepping the news desk while Linda did microphone sound checks and adjusted the lighting. No one even noticed me there.

"I went into the makeup area, where Stephanie had just finished hair and makeup on Jean, the evening news co-anchor, and was about to start on Jeff. Jean was the station's first female co-anchor and was a total professional. Jeff was also a professional, but he was much more comfortable and joked around a lot, both on camera and off. He kept the newsroom calm, but everyone knew he had his sights set on national news.

"Everything was going smoothly, so rather than get in the way, I decided to go to the storage room and pick out the equipment I needed for my reindeer remote. The camera I chose was a smaller version of the standup remotes we used in the fields. It was a lot smaller and lighter. I picked out two lenses, one for low light conditions and a telephoto lens. I added two rechargeable batteries to ensure I had enough filming time to last four hours. The camera I picked used mini recording tapes, and I put six new high-resolution cartridges in my supplies. The last things I grabbed were an adjustable tripod, a shoulder strap for easy carrying, and two carrying cases.

"I carefully packed my cases but then realized I had forgotten the battery charger, which I added to the pile.

"As I was leaving the studio, I crossed paths with John on his way

The Legend of Stormy and the Great Northern Christmas Spirit & Tree Company

to the production booth. He shook my hand and wished me luck, and as he was walking away, he turned back and said, 'Be careful up there, and don't take any unnecessary risks.'

"I got a chill all over my body and felt the hairs on the back of my neck stand up. This was two people who said the exact same thing. I was glad Scott offered to walk me to my car. He carried the bigger of the bags, and as he loaded it in my trunk, he turned to me, smiled, and said, 'You got this, kid; have fun with it, and I'll see you when you get back.' He headed back into the station. I got into my car and took a deep breath, let it out slowly, and repeated his words to myself: 'You got this, kid; you got this.'

"I don't really remember the drive back to the apartment, but when I arrived, I unpacked the trunk and went inside. I put the camera equipment on the bedroom floor next to the white snow boots and picked up the envelope with the brochures, my tickets, and my itinerary. I went into the living room and sat down on the couch. I turned on the TV and switched it to channel 5.

"The lead story was the weather. It seems a winter storm was building in the Pacific; Jeff turned it over to our meteorologist, Rick Roberson.

"Rick was a tall man who always wore a white shirt with a dark tie. He had been at the station longer than anyone else, even John, and he was very popular in the community. He showed the latest maps and described the weather patterns in the Northwest. The storm was coming very early for that part of the Pacific and could affect a large part of the western United States, all the way from northern California to most parts of Alaska and into western Canada. Rick said he would be keeping a close eye on the storm's progress and should have a better idea of its strength later in the week. He said he would have more on this later in the broadcast, but now he sent it over to Jean.

"Jean said we were all looking forward to his updates, adding, 'One of our own, camerawoman Miss Jane [my picture appeared briefly on the screen], was soon to be heading to Alaska for a holiday feature on the migration of reindeer.'

"Jeff said, 'We wish her a safe trip, and Miss Jane, if you're watching, be careful, and don't take any unnecessary risks up there.'

"Once again, the hairs on the back of my neck stood up, and the chills returned. I turned the TV off, shut my eyes, took another deep breath, and muttered to myself, 'You got this, kid.' I stood up and got a glass of water from the kitchen sink, sat back down, and looked at my itinerary. When I looked at the dates, I froze. I must not have been listening when Crystal told me the dates and times of my trip because I was scheduled to fly out of Detroit the day after tomorrow. It was an early flight, and Crystal had booked a room for me at the airport hotel in Detroit for tomorrow, with a check-in time of 3 p.m. Time was already short, so I went in and started packing.

"I didn't get much sleep that night. Susan called me the next morning to make sure I had everything I needed. I told her I did and thanked her; after I hung the phone up, I realized this was real. This was happening. I spent the rest of the morning going over everything again and again. I decided I would leave for Detroit at one o'clock, and one o'clock came a lot sooner than it usually does, or at least it felt that way to me. I packed my car and went over all my lists one more time. The drive to Detroit was reasonably uneventful. I checked into the hotel, went to my room, and ordered room service and a wake-up call.

"I ate quickly, and when I was done, I turned the TV on and lay down. I must have fallen right to sleep because the next thing I knew, I was awoken by the phone. It was my wake-up call. I had slept straight through the night. I got dressed, checked out of the room, and caught a shuttle bus to the terminal. I checked my bags, everything but the camera bag, which I kept with me, and found my way to my gate. I took a seat facing the runway and waited for the boarding to begin.

"As I sat there watching the other planes take off and land, it hit me: I never even told my mom and dad I was going on this trip. I looked around the terminal, saw a payphone, and called them. The answering machine picked up; I hesitated a second and then told them what was going on. I told them I loved them and said I'd call as soon as I got the chance. Finally, I told them I'd try to make it home for Christmas. Then I hung up.

"I remember crying some and feeling all alone. The PA announced the boarding was beginning for my flight. I gathered up my camera bag and got in line.

"After everyone was on the plane, which was only about half-full, the stewardesses gave the seat belt, oxygen mask, and emergency exit talk. The captian, he said his name was Shawn Shiffer or Shaffer or something like that, came on the intercom and said we were first in line for take-off. He said the weather was good all the way to Minneapolis and to enjoy the flight. I shut my eyes and said a little prayer, and we were off.

"The landing in Minneapolis was as smooth as the take-off from Detroit. I waited my turn to leave the plane, entered the Minneapolis airport, and found my way to the next gate."

Chapter 10

❦

I hadn't really noticed, but Grandma had been talking for almost an hour. The story was so interesting that I didn't even mind. I couldn't wait to hear what happened in Alaska, but for now, I just drank my cocoa and listened on.

* * *

"The plane to Anchorage was noticeably smaller but still only about half-full. I had a row of seats all to myself, so after we took off, I lifted the armrests and stretched out. I must have fallen right asleep because the stewardess, whose name tag read 'Nichole,' nudged my feet and asked if I wanted anything to eat.

I was super hungry. The last time I had eaten was the night before in the airport hotel, so I ordered the beef tips in noodles over gravy and a pop.

Nichole looked at me a little strangely and asked what a pop was.

I said, "You know, a cola."

She laughed and said, "You mean a soda?"

Yes, a soda is what I meant. It turns out only Midwesterners call it a pop. Like I said, I hadn't traveled much up to this point. I looked out my window while I was waiting for my food; all I could see were snowcapped mountains. It was beautiful. I stood up, opened the overhead compartment, and pulled my camera bag out. I removed the video camera, took the lens cap off, and started shooting footage straight out of my window.

This was the first time I experienced turbulence. The plane jumped and bumped, and the camera eyepiece smacked my eye. I turned it off and set it back in the bag just about the same time Nichole came on the intercom, announced that the captain had turned the seat belt sign back on, and said everyone should return to their seats. I tightened my belt and shut my eyes.

Nichole brought my food and asked me if I'd like her to put my bag back in the overhead bin. I said yes. The plane smoothed back out. The seat belt sign went off, and I ate my beef tips and noodles in gravy. I lay back down and fell asleep again.

I woke up to another round of turbulence and put my seat belt on. This time, I made sure it was real tight. The captain came over the intercom once again and announced the rest of the flight was going to be bumpy. He suggested if we needed a restroom break, we should go now. I didn't need to use the restroom before he mentioned it, but I really needed to go now. I guess the power of suggestion is a force to be reckoned with, because when I came out, there was a line at both the front and rear restrooms. I bumped my way back to my seat, buckled in, and prepared to ride it out.

We were only an hour and a half from Anchorage, and I was ready to get off this plane. We bumped and dipped all the way there, and when it came time to land, all the passengers, including myself, were completely silent. I'm not sure if we felt being quiet would help the pilot and copilot concentrate or if, like me, everyone was just too nervous to talk.

Nichole and the other two stewardesses made one last trip through the cabin collecting trash, checking seat belts, and making sure that our seatbacks and tray tables were in their full upright position. As Nichole passed my row, she glanced my way and said, with what she must have thought was a reassuring smile, "We're fine, piece of cake."

I might have found some comfort in that statement if she didn't have so much fear and doubt in her eyes. When I looked out my window, all I could see was white. It was a total whiteout; the plane jumped and rocked like it could be ripped apart at any time, and all I could think about was that I would never get my feature spot on the five o'clock news, not that I hadn't talked to my parents before I left or that I wouldn't make it home by Christmas or that we might just crash on landing. No, all I thought about was I wasn't going to get my two minutes of airtime on a medium-size TV station in a medium-size market in rural Indiana.

"This is probably when I should have taken a look at my priorities, but I had waited and worked for this opportunity since I was a sophomore in high school in that small video club, with Miss Penny showing the way to a promising and exciting future."

* * *

Grandma's phone rang, and it startled me. It was almost like being awoken from a dream. I jumped a little as Dad got up to answer it. I was so caught up in Grandma's story, I forgot where I was and what we were doing. I realized it was still December 21, and we were finishing up the tree (well, it was done except for lighting up the stupid reindeer on the top).

I heard Dad say, "Good, let me get, Ma" and he called Grandma into the kitchen. She looked at me and must have been able to tell from my expression I wanted to hear more of her story because she winked at me, held up one finger, and walked to the kitchen.

She took the phone from Dad and said, "That's good … I understand … no, not yet … of course we'll wait. See you then, love you, be careful, bye bye." Then she hung up.

She grabbed the plate of cookies that was on the counter and brought them back into the living room with her. Dad grabbed two or three of them, and so did I. Even Grandma took one for herself. They were sugar cookies we had baked earlier in the day. We had frosted them with her famous homemade frosting. She could whip up a bowl of it in about fifteen minutes, add some food coloring, and be ready to decorate cookies by the time they were cool enough to eat. We used her old cookie cutters to create shapes of bells, Christmas trees, and Santa Claus with his bag of toys slung over his shoulder. The cookie cutters were

The Legend of Stormy and the Great Northern Christmas Spirit & Tree Company

another thing that came in an old wooden box with those same fancy red words on sides, *The Great Northern Christmas Spirit & Tree Co.*

I took a big bite of one of the Santa cookies, drank some cocoa, and waited for the story to continue.

Grandma said, "Now, where was I?" and I blurted out, "In the plane, during a snowstorm, getting ready to land in Alaska."

She looked at me a bit surprised. Maybe she was surprised that I had been paying such close attention or that I wanted to hear more; I'm not sure which it was, but she looked surprised, nonetheless.

"Yes, yes, that's right," she began, and I had already forgotten that the phone had rung and interrupted the story in the first place.

Chapter 11

❦

"As I was saying, we were coming in for the landing; the plane was jumping and dipping violently. I could feel my seat belt cutting into my waist. My head jerked up and down and then left and right. I couldn't control my arms or legs, and they flailed like a rag doll thrown out a window. I remember hearing the woman behind me trying to comfort her son, who was crying at this point, and I could tell she was crying too.

"There were gasps and moans coming from everywhere in the cabin as the plane lurched again, first to the left and then back to the right. The plane felt like it was flying sideways, and then came the screams.

"I couldn't figure out why everyone was screaming. *Why scream?* I thought. *What would that help?* As that thought ran through my mind, I realized I was screaming too. Some of the overhead compartments came open, and their contents spilled out into the aisle. The cabin lights flickered once, twice, and then they seemed to go out altogether, but they didn't. As it turned out, it was just me blinking and then closing my eyes. I crouched down into the crash position and held my breath. When I held my breath, I also held my screams. Everyone else must have been doing the same thing because the plane became deadly quiet. Nothing but a few gasps and some sobbing and the sound of the engines fighting for control.

"That's when it happened: The whole world became still. The engines quieted back down, and the jerking and bobbing stopped. I felt like I was floating in thin air. The calm was even more frightening than the jerks and bumps. I raised my head and looked out my window, and I could see lights. At first, I couldn't figure out what they were, but they were bright and focused, all red, green, and white. The white ones blinked on and off in a distinct pattern, and I realized what I was seeing: It was a runway. The snow had stopped, or we had out run it or finally dipped below it. Other passengers were sitting up now too, all of them looking around, shocked, confused, but still completely silent.

"We banked a pretty hard right and then leveled out, and the plane set down on the runway with a soft thud. The brakes were applied, and the engines roared. The plane slowed quickly and smoothly, and we were just taxiing along. The next thing I heard was the captain on the intercom, saying, 'Welcome to Alaska.'

"Cheers exploded throughout the entire cabin, and there was a round of laughter, not the kind laughter you hear when someone tells a funny joke or story, but the kind you hear when crying is the only other alternative. On the way to the gate, the captain thanked us for flying with them and thanked the crew for the fine job they had done.

"The plane finally stopped, and the jet engines shut down; they opened the door, and I could feel cold air rush in. It was a welcome feeling because I was still hot from fear-induced adrenaline. My clothes were damp with perspiration. Everyone stood up at once. We looked around and nodded to each other. I could tell that we had been bonded together by this experience forever, even though we would probably never see one another again. I turned and embraced the woman who had been sitting behind me, and her son hugged me out of nowhere. I hugged him back as if he were my son too.

"I reached up into the overhead compartment and retrieved my camera bag, which I half-expected to be torn apart with the camera shattered in pieces, only to find it was just as I had left it. I grabbed it and started down the aisle toward the door; when I finally reached the front of the plane, Nichole was standing by the exit.

"She looked me right in the eye and with the same smile as before said, 'Piece of cake.' Her eyes were red, and her makeup was smeared under both eyes. I was pretty sure it wasn't from perspiring. We both laughed, and I gave her a hug and left the plane.

"The airport was small compared to Detroit and Minneapolis. It didn't have an enclosed walkway into the terminal. We walked down a set of metal stairs that was pushed up to the door and right onto the snow-covered tarmac. The cold hit me like jumping into a swimming pool in late May. It took my breath away, and I could feel it all the way into my bones. At this point, I was sure glad I had gone crazy in the military surplus store with all the long johns, gloves, boots, and stuff.

"I went to the restroom and splashed water on my face to refresh me from the less-than-smooth trip this far. After I exited the restroom, I looked for a departure monitor to see when the final flight of this adventure was scheduled to leave. The screen showed most of the flights that were heading south and east and back to the real world were either delayed or canceled. I assumed this was due to the storm we had just flown through. I guess Rick the weatherman was dead-on with his forecast. I was really hoping he would be wrong, at least this time.

"My flight to Fairbanks was still on time, so I went to the gate and once again took a seat that looked out onto the runway. The snow was coming down lightly for now, but the view in the distance told a story of big changes coming. The crowd at the gate was pretty sparse, and I wondered if we would end up delayed waiting for more passengers to arrive. The airport was nearly deserted, except for about ten people who were waiting with me. An announcement came over the PA saying flight 1980 to Fairbanks would be boarding shortly. The people around me started to get up, collect their possessions, and shuffle toward the gate door. I followed along.

"I handed my ticket to the clerk and walked out into the frigid air, climbing down the steps leading to the tarmac. I followed an older gentleman who was wearing a hat similar to the one I had bought for my trip, only much older and weathered than mine. He was rather short but still had a healthy stride. He had a scruffy beard but a pleasant face, and his eyes seemed to smile at you. It looked to me like he could have been a gold miner or fur trapper or something. We walked straight ahead to my worst nightmare.

"Twenty-five feet away sat a little twin-engine plane with the door opened down to make a set of steps, four in all. As I climbed those four small steps, I was greeted by the copilot sitting in the right-hand seat of the plane, with the captain sitting to his left, wearing a headset and checking a mess of gauges on the dashboard. I could see right out the windshield, although I didn't want to. The small plane only had nine rows of seats, with one on each side of a narrow aisle. There was a small door in the back of the plane with a lighted sign above it that simple read, RESTROOM. I was hoping I wouldn't need to use that door.

"I sat in the third row on the pilot side of the plane, behind the man with the beard and the weathered hat. He seemed completely at ease with this form of transportation. From my seat, I could still see out the windshield and decided to keep my eyes down during the takeoff. I was even surer I would close them completely at the landing, if we made it that far.

"The door closed, the engines roared to life, and we were on our way. After a short taxi to the runway, the pilot gunned the engines, and the small plane quickly picked up speed, lifted off, and climbed steeply. It felt much different from the jets I was just on, and the ride was a lot rougher than the heavier planes too. We flew without incident all the way to Fairbanks, and I became pretty comfortable with the plane. I even watched the landing right out the windshield, even though I swore I wouldn't. The airport in Fairbanks was even smaller than the one in Anchorage, but it had a friendly welcoming look and feel to it. We exited the plane, and though I didn't think it was possible, it was even colder here. I ran with my camera bag into the airport and soaked in the warmth. It only took ten minutes to collect the rest of my bags, and I headed for the exit, where I was to meet my contact for the rest of my journey."

Chapter 12

❦

"Just inside the exit door," Grandma continued, "the gray-haired man with the scruffy beard and smiling eyes looked right at me and produced a small cardboard sign with my name on it, written in a very distinct and old-looking script. It simply said 'JANE,' but the red letters seemed to say more. I walked up to him and asked if I knew him, and he said he was hired by a TV station out of Indiana to escort a young woman named Jane, who was there to film the reindeer migration.

"I told him that was me, and once again his eyes smiled at me. He said his name was Earl. He helped me with my bags (not the camera bag; I carried that one myself). Normally, I wouldn't have left with a stranger, especially in a land as remote and different as Alaska, but I felt like I had known Earl all my life and had no fear of being with him.

"We left the warmth and safety of the airport and walked out to a small parking lot, with only ten or twelve vehicles in it. All were big pickups. Some were newer than the others, but all of them looked worn from either the rough winters or maybe poorly maintained roads. We walked in the dangerous and bitter cold; I had pulled out my new gloves and hat, the hat that nearly matched Earl's, only newer, and put them on. They didn't help much, but it was better than nothing.

"As we walked to the parking lot, I couldn't help but think if anyone was looking at us, they would have thought we were family of some sort, maybe a granddaughter visiting her lonely old grandfather for the holidays or something. Nothing could have been further from the truth, but we see what we want to see. Even though I knew we weren't related, the thought brought me some comfort.

"We passed a nice Chevy pickup with a cap over the bed and then two Ford four-wheel drive models that were also pretty nice and ended up at a beat-up truck with dents in the back bumper and a large scrape down the passenger side. The rims on the passenger side were different colors; the front one was gray, and the rear one was a faded and slightly rusted black. Earl gently set my bags in the bed of the pickup, which already contained some pine needles and several boxes, the contents of which I didn't ask about (partly because it was none of my business but mostly because I was afraid of what might have been in them), and opened my door for me. The old truck's interior lights didn't work, but the cab was clean, and the seat, at least my side, was barely worn. I pushed my camera bag into the middle and climbed in.

"Earl shut the door behind me. I felt around for the seat belt but was unable to find one, and Earl ambled in on the driver's side. He moved like a man much younger than his outward appearance. Once he had his door shut, he stepped on a button on the floor by his left foot, and the motor roared to life. He saw me looking for the seat belt and smiled; he said he was sorry but this old truck didn't come with seat belts. He did say that he would be careful; I'm not sure if it was to reassure me or tease me, but he added that he hardly ever hits too many things, anyway.

"He chuckled to himself and put the truck in gear, and we were off. That's when I remembered the dent on the bumper and the scratch down my side of the truck and pressed my feet hard against the floorboards; his smile grew a little bit bigger, and his laugh became a bit louder. I think I laughed too at that point, but not the kind of laugh that said something was funny; the other kind, the kind I had shared with the passengers on the plane just after landing for the first time in Alaska.

"Earl didn't speak for the first few minutes, and neither did I. Finally, he looked over at me and asked if I knew my agenda for the next couple of days. It was at that point I realized I had no idea what the plan was. I didn't even know where I was going to be staying or who would be contacting me when I got there. Heck, I didn't even know where or what I was going to be eating while I was here, but now that

I was thinking about it, I was really hungry and could use a drink of water or a pop, sorry soda, or something.

"Earl seemed to read my mind and said if it was all right with me, he wanted to stop at a diner at the edge of town for some food before we continued on. I told him it sounded good to me and I could probably stand for a bite or two, and again he laughed, and this time, I laughed with him, a real laugh, and it felt comforting.

"We stopped at a place simply named the Diner. We slid out of the truck, and with our matching hats, we entered the diner and were greeted by a young woman, younger than me even, with short blonde hair, a sweet smile, and two menus in hand. I noticed she was wearing two different colors of knee-high stockings and short fur-lined black leather boots. She introduced herself as Heather and led us to a table near the center of the dining area, not too close to the door and not too close to the kitchen, but just close enough to the big stone fireplace that I got a cozy and homey feeling.

"Heather poured Earl a large cup of coffee, even though he didn't ask for one, and brought me a glass of ice water. She left us with our menus and our drinks. I asked Earl if he came here a lot, and he said he stops in from time to time if he has business in town.

"Heather came back with some plates, silverware, and two napkins; topped off Earl's coffee; and asked if we were ready. I ordered a turkey club sandwich and chips. Earl ordered a burger and fries and some pie. I asked her if they had any sodas, and Heather let out a little laugh and nodded her head. I added a cola. Heather thanked us, pulled some ketchup and mustard from her apron, and set them on the table before heading for the kitchen.

"I looked around and only saw two other groups with us. One group was another older man and woman and a small child. The child I figured was a granddaughter because she had similar features as the couple and was very comfortable with them, but they seemed too old to have such a young child.

"I took the still camera out of my bag and snapped a shot of them out of habit. Then I took a picture of Earl. The view out the window behind him was a perfect backdrop. The other group looked like hunters. They wore camouflage jackets and red caps. They talked among themselves and seemed oblivious to anyone else being in the diner.

"Earl said that after we were done eating, we would head to North Pole and get set for the night. He said when I get settled in, I should try to get some sleep because tomorrow was going to be a big day. I asked what was going on tomorrow, and he told me if I was going to get any footage of the caribou, it would have to be tomorrow, and it would have to be early because of the limited light. There was a big storm coming, and it looked to be a doozie.

"I asked him how I would contact my guide or my pilot or whoever. He said not to worry; he had taken care of all that. I asked where I would be staying, and he said Crystal had set me up with a nice cabin for the time that I would be here. He said it was just down the road from what he called Santa's House. I wondered if Santa's House was just a local joke and tourist trap or what, but I guess I would soon find out. I asked how big this town of North Pole was and how far away it was; Earl said it was a nice little town, and we were on the outskirts of it right now.

"Our food came, and we ate without talking anymore. After I finished my sandwich and drank some of my cola, Heather returned and cleared my plate. Earl was just about done, and Heather had his pie with her. He slid his cup over to her, and she refilled it. The pie was peach, and it smelled so good, I ordered one too. She brought it right back and took Earl's burger plate.

"I asked Earl if he lived here, and he said not really but that his brother Nickolas did. He said the family business kept him very busy and that he spent most of his time traveling. Earl said he was kind of a silent partner with his brother, and it kept him busy and on the move. He also said he came here every year at this time on business and to visit family and friends. We finished our pie; I paid the check and left a generous tip, and we were on our way out the door. Heather waved goodbye, and back out into the brutal cold we went.

"We climbed back into the truck; Earl started it up, and down the road we went. We drove through town on snow-covered roads lined with evergreen trees and a few houses. The houses were very modest but seemed well kept. Smoke rose from the chimneys, and dull red light spewed from the slits in the curtains covering the windows. A lone moose the size of a large horse, with a wide full rack, ambled down the middle of the road. Earl slowed the truck and let the moose continue down the road without bothering it. Finally, it just walked off into the forest and disappeared as if it wasn't even there to begin with. I did manage to get some good shots of it before it disappeared into the trees.

"After driving a few miles, there was a sign at the side of the road that said 'Welcome to North Pole, Alaska: Home of Santa's Castle.' I looked at Earl, and he seemed to read my mind. 'Yes, Santa's Castle,' he said, but his smile told me he knew I wasn't buying it. As we continued through town, I shot more stills and took some video. We passed a few other trucks and even a couple snow machines, what I called snowmobiles, and there it was, off to the left side of the road: Santa's Castle. It looked more like a storefront from a strip mall than a castle, but it was there, nonetheless. Earl stopped just short of it, and I took several more pictures. When he sensed I was done taking my pictures, he continued on. The tires slipped on the snow, and I could feel all four dig in. I was glad we at least had four-wheel drive on the old truck."

Chapter 13

❧

"A mile or so further down the road," Grandma said, "Earl made a right turn into the woods and followed a narrow road. This road was more like a lane or a driveway than an actual road. It wound through the trees for maybe half a mile and opened into a large clearing. At the far end of the clearing was a log cabin. The cabin had smoke rising from a chimney that stood in the center of the roof. The front porch was made of rough knotted pine trees with a large overhang. The cabin door was directly in the middle of the porch about ten feet from the steps and nestled between two windows. The same red glow crept out between the gaps in the curtains, and it gave the whole place a warm, welcoming feeling. The porch wrapped around the entire front of the cabin, spilling around the sides and out of sight. The six steps leading up to the porch were about seven feet in width, with handrails made of the same knotty pine connected to posts going out both sides and framing the porch. There was fresh snow all around; it was so smooth, it appeared to have been painted or sprayed there rather than fallen from the sky.

"The lights from the truck shown into the distance, and I could tell the whole compound was encircled in the same pine trees I had seen since we left the airport. They were all of different sizes and types. Some were very tall and wide with small needles and thin branches, while others were just three or four feet tall and had longer and thicker needles.

"As we swung to the left, my side of the truck faced the porch. I noticed a large building off in the trees. It looked like a large barn, but it was low to the ground. The roof was only maybe fifteen feet off the ground, and it had to be forty feet wide. The barn or whatever it was didn't have any windows in the front, and I didn't see any chimney on the roof. It was all dark and looked like it was used for some type of storage, not for living in. When Earl stopped the truck, the headlights settled onto the front of the barn and showed a long door that ran almost all the way from one end to the other and was nearly as tall as the barn itself. I didn't see any other entrance to the structure but assumed that there must be a door on one of the sides.

"Earl shut the truck off, opened his door, and stepped out. The cold air flooded into the cab, and I was reminded that all the beauty I saw was encased in the extreme cold that was winter in Alaska. I put my camera in its case, pulled on my gloves, and opened my door. Earl met me as I exited the old truck and helped me with my suitcase and the rest of my stuff from the bed of the truck. He led me up the steps and onto the porch. The snow crunched under our feet, and the sound echoed through the trees.

"For the first time since arriving in Alaska, I noticed the smell. All the pine trees, with their many different types and lengths of needles, filled the air with a sweet, comforting smell. I wasn't sure how to describe it, but all I could think was it made me feel like a kid again, back home with my family, peaceful and happy. Maybe it was just the cold air or the near-deafening quiet, but whatever it was, I felt a calm come over me. It was a feeling that I hadn't felt in a long, long time.

"Earl opened the door to the cabin, and warmth spilled out onto the porch. He took all my stuff in, and I followed. I shut the door; the only light in the cabin came from the large fireplace that was set on the right wall near the center of the room.

"The room was spacious and set in a backwards L shape. The right side with the fireplace ran about twenty-five feet to the entrance of the kitchen area. I could see a small dining table and a counter from my position near the door. From the fireplace wall to the left wall was fifteen feet or so, and the left wall was ten feet long, with a door directly across from the fireplace. The wall facing me and running left to the end of the house was fifteen to eighteen feet long and also had a door nearly halfway down it. I guessed these two doors were bedroom doors. The left wall that ran back up to the front wall had a single window in it; the curtains were closed, but I imagined it faced directly at the barn I saw as we parked.

"The furniture in the cabin was rustic looking. There was an old bentwood-style rocking chair with a quilt over it near the left wall window. It had a small wooden table on its right side and a magazine rack on its left. A couch was centered under the front window facing the old rocker, with a small table in front of it matching the wooden table next to the rocker. After my long trip, they both looked inviting to me.

"Earl went into the kitchen and turned on a light. He came back and opened the door across from the fireplace and carried my belongings in. Another light came on, and he called me into the room.

"'This will be your room,' he said. I looked around, and the only things in the room were a small double bed, a wooden dresser with four drawers, and a nightstand, which held the light. There were no windows and no closet. This was truly the basics.

"Earl walked out, and I followed him into the kitchen. It was smaller than I thought it would be. A small wooden table occupied much of the area. The counter was short, and on the left side was a small sink with a low faucet and mismatched towels and washrags draped over the edge. A small bathroom was off to one side. The bathroom was clean and neat, with a pedestal-style sink with a mirror above it and a toilet on its left. The toilet paper roll sat on the tank of the toilet. Across from the toilet was an enclosed shower, and next to it was a linen closet with towels, washcloths, and spare toilet paper. The only room left in the cabin I figured must have been Earl's bedroom.

"I put the rest of my stuff into my room. As I was unpacking, I could hear some rustling and clanging.

"The clanging I was hearing was an old metal pan and a large metal spoon. I unpacked and put all my things in the small dresser. I was laying out my clothes for the next day when the scent drifted into my room, a scent that was familiar, like an old dream. It was sweet and thick and comforting all at the same time. I continued setting out my wardrobe. I chose the long johns and thick socks. I added a sweatshirt, the white parka with the white fur on the hood and sleeves, and last but not least, the white rubber boots with the valves on the sides. I looked at it lying across the bed and thought it looked like a deflated snowman from a bad movie or something. I laughed at myself and went out to the kitchen to see what Earl was making.

"I saw him hunched over the stove with a pan on the burner. He was slowly stirring a batch of cocoa with a large spoon. He slowly and carefully stirred it counterclockwise, and the steam rose and filled the room with the sweetness. He asked me to get two large cups out of the cupboard above the sink. I opened the door and pulled two large cups with fancy red script on them. The script looked very old, as did the cups themselves. The script said 'The Great Northern Christmas Spirit & Tree Co.' I sat the cups on the counter next to an old metal canister with a round metal lid. It had the same writing on it. I asked Earl what the Great Northern Christmas Spirit & Tree Co. was, and he turned to me and smiled.

With a gleam in his eye, he said, 'It's a small family business my brother and I started a long time ago. We saw a need for a change in the world and just decided to create something special. It was really small and regional at first but now has grown to be worldwide.'

"He removed the pan from the stove and turned it off. He filled the cups with the cocoa straight from the pan and opened a drawer to his left. The cocoa's sweet smell filled my mind with thoughts of my childhood and cold December nights back in northwest Ohio where I was born and grew up before moving to Indiana for college and my job at WXMAS. My mom would make us hot chocolate, and we would sit around and discuss the day's events before going to bed. It brought me back to a much simpler time, when life was just about family, and everything seemed safe and right. Once again, I began to feel guilty about being away from my family at this special time of the year, and for the first time in years, I longed for home.

"This cocoa was even sweeter than my mom's, I could tell, and I hadn't even tasted it yet. Earl took a bag of miniature marshmallows from the drawer; he counted out eight marshmallows for each cup and dropped them in, one at a time. We picked up our cups. Earl grabbed two spoons from the same drawer that held the bag of marshmallows, and we went into the living room. The fire cracked in the fireplace as we walked by, almost as if it was planned, and we sat down.

"Earl sat on the wooden rocker and put his cup on the table on his right, and I sat on the couch and held my cup. We stirred the cocoa, and Earl took a sip, closed his eyes, and smiled like he was thinking of something happy, from his past maybe. I went to take a sip and looked into the cup as I raised it to my lips, and I swear the marshmallows had formed into four rows of two. It seemed odd, but once the sweet cocoa touched my lips, I closed my eyes and felt safe and right at home."

* * *

I found myself looking down into my cocoa while Grandma continued her story. I had to assume it was coincidence, but my marshmallows were also formed into four distinct rows of two. I took a sip, closed my eyes, and listened on.

* * *

Grandma continued, "Nick and Earl were what was known as woodsmen. They chopped down trees for lumber and firewood. 'It was a good life,' he said. 'We worked for a good company and were proud of our jobs. We supplied the local community with lumber to build their homes and businesses and wood for their fireplaces to give them heat in the cold winters. That is when things began to change. There was a large migration of people. The demand became great. Our company struggled to keep up with this demand and was taken over by a bigger company from out of the area. The new company started to strip the forests in the name of profit and didn't care about the damage they were doing. They just kept cutting and cutting. They cut everything. They cut the big trees, they cut the little trees, and they even cut the saplings that would regenerate the forest. This went on for nearly a year; we could see the damage it was doing to the beautiful forests we knew and loved. We shared our concerns with our new boss; he told us that we were here for a job, and if we didn't like how things were going, we could leave.

"'We left,' Earl continued. 'We headed north and west, picking up odd jobs as we traveled till we arrived here. It was midfall, and we were warned the winter would come soon, and it would be harsh, harsher than anything we had ever experienced in our lives, and if we weren't prepared, we wouldn't survive it. We took our savings and purchased a large piece of land north of where we are now and started clearing it a little at a time, using the lumber we cleared to build a two-room cabin. We stocked up on supplies and finished the cabin just as the first snows came. We hunkered down and rode the winter out. And what a winter it was. The cold was bitter, and the snow, after it started, never seemed to stop. It was dark twenty-three hours a day, and the sun never really came up; it just lit the sky to the east for an hour, and then it was gone again. We ran low on everything and were sure we would not survive, just like we were told. Luckily, the snow soon stopped. The days started getting longer, and we even started seeing the sun again. As it warmed up, we were able to get out and resupply ourselves.

"'We started working again as soon as we could, and we felt things were going to be all right. The first year was rough, but we managed. We started to clear more land close to the cabin. We opened up the front area in a circle and left the saplings to keep the woods healthy and sustainable.

"'Some of the local people came by and offered to help us,' he said. 'We became good friends with our neighbors. They all had different skills. Some were bakers; some were blacksmiths. There were cooks and candy makers, farmers and clothes makers, and even a shoemaker who worked with all types of leather. They, like us, were just trying to survive and make a living for themselves and their families. We all used our skills and resources to help each other, and it was going well. When one family needed boots for their children, then the shoemaker would make them, and instead of being paid in money, they would trade their skill to help out another, who would do the same till everyone was able to survive, and we all prospered. We had a small community, a small town, as it were. We were a community set apart from the rest of the world and yet still connected and influenced by that world's need and greed. What started as pure fellowship was returning to the status quo.

The Legend of Stormy and the Great Northern Christmas Spirit & Tree Company

Nick and I were talking one evening about how we were letting our values fade, and he said this was a good life but not what we sacrificed for. He wanted to do so much more for so many more but was afraid that without a structure we could control or influence, we would just end up like the world we left not long ago.

"'We called a meeting of the townsfolk and shared our concerns. We asked for ideas of how to preserve what we had built. The first to speak up was Greg. Greg is a miner and supplies us with the gold, silver, and many of the metals and jewels we use. He said if we somehow created a business, we could bring our products to the world without bringing the world to us, and that way, we could go on doing what each of us does best and still manage to be self-sufficient and maybe even show the rest of the world you can help others without taking advantage of them. He said if we did it right, maybe it would bring hope and joy to people everywhere.

"'Everyone agreed this was a good idea,' Grandma said Earl explained, 'but no one knew how to go about doing it. So we discussed it well into the night. Each group offered to use their skills and abilities to help form the company, but no one knew what the product would be. Out of nowhere came a suggestion from a young farmer named Logan. Logan was normally very quiet and kept to himself, but he stood up and said we should start a company that brought hope instead of material goods. At first, many in the group laughed, but the more they thought about it, the better the idea became to them. Others in the group began to ask him what he meant, and he said if we took our skills and worked together, we could provide the world with things that made them think of each other rather than themselves. He said that we could create a line of products under one company name that reminded people of times spent together as families, just like we do here. The problem was what kind of a business would fulfill this idea. Logan said it could be a Christmas company.

"'The meeting went completely silent,' Earl said. 'No one said a word; they just looked at each other. Then Nick looked right at Logan and smiled. That smile was all that the people needed to see. Someone near the back started to clap, and then more and more joined in, and just as quickly as the silence came, so did the cheers. Even though we didn't know what it meant to start a Christmas company, we all decided to form one.

"'There was an agreement among the entire group that Nick would lead the company. Over the next few months, representatives from each of the families, with their different skills and abilities, met with Nick, and together, they came up with a list of products to make and decided on a name for the company. The name agreed upon was the Great Northern Christmas Spirit & Tree Co. We have had great success and have expanded the company many times. The cocoa you are drinking is one of the first products we distributed and has become a favorite throughout the ages.'

"As Earl was telling the story about the Great Northern Christmas Spirit & Tree Co., I was getting tired," Grandma said. "I wasn't sure if it was the warm fire crackling in the background, the long trip across the country, or the sweet hot cocoa, but I was having trouble keeping my eyes open. I yawned out loud, and Earl stopped his story and smiled at me. He got up and refilled our cups one last time and politely suggested we turn in for the night. He said that it was getting late and we had an early day tomorrow, so I thanked him for everything and headed to my room. I put on my pajamas and climbed into the bed. It was soft, and the covers were warm and comforting, all at the same time. I don't even remember closing my eyes, and I was fast asleep. I dreamed of the snow and the cocoa and even dreamed about the moose that was blocking the road earlier. My dreams came nonstop throughout the night, and what was odd is I don't remember having dreams of any type since I started college, maybe even since high school.

"Even though I knew I was sleeping and the dreams were probably just caused by all the excitement and new surroundings, I remembered thinking that I hoped it would go on forever."

Chapter 14

"I was startled out of sleep by a loud noise," Grandma continued. "I was still half-dreaming and mostly asleep, and the noise worked its way into my unconsciousness. It alerted me that a change was happening. I needed to wake up and investigate its source. I fought to keep the comfortable sleep the dreams had provided, but the noise became louder and clearer. Finally, my eyes popped open. At first, I struggled to understand where I was and why I was here, but I remembered the whole thing, the assignment, the trip, Earl, Alaska, and the reindeer. Even though it was cold now, I took the mug I had left on the stand next to my bed and sipped my cocoa again."

* * *

I started to think about my own dreams. I remember having dreams like Grandma talked about. Dreams about horses running wild in fields filled with flowers so colorful, so vivid they brought tears to my mind's eye. Flowers so real I believed I could smell them. The smells those flowers produced filled my dreams with melodies and songs familiar and yet unknown.

I remember dreams of swinging in the back yard of the little house I grew up in and going so high, I thought I would drift off into space.

There were also dreams of Christmas, and the one I remember most was about a reindeer. I was riding on this reindeer and traveling across the whole world. I saw the lights below me and heard the bells the reindeer wore jingling as we swooped and rose up into the stars and back to earth. My dreams were a fun and safe fantasy that filled my sleep. As I grew older, my dreams changed. They turned into more serious subjects and became more of an interruption than a comfort during sleep. They were filled with things like the fear of an upcoming test or mismatched clothes and bad hair days. The dreams I loved came less and less frequently, and sometimes, they didn't come at all. I miss the dreams of my childhood but figured it was all part of growing up.

As I thought about my dreams, Grandma continued.

* * *

"I hopped out of the bed," she said, "put on my robe, and went out into the living room. The fireplace was still burning strong, and the smell of sweet cocoa hung in the air, but Earl was nowhere to be seen. It appeared to still be dark outside, but I couldn't tell for sure because the curtains were closed. The noise that had stolen my beautiful sleep and interrupted my dreams still filled my ears, and now my curiosity was taking control of my thoughts.

"I went to the window at the end of the living room next to Earl's bedroom door, pushed aside the curtains, and found it was still dark, indeed. The large barn with the long door in the front was lit on the inside, and light was spilling out through the open door. The snow glowed from the light and illuminated the whole open space. It spread all the way to the evergreen trees surrounding the property. I could see a shadow moving in the entrance to the barn and decided to get dressed and see what was going on. I went back to my room and started pulling on all the things I had bought at the surplus store. I put on the warm socks and then the long johns. I added my slacks and then my ski pants. I pulled on my air boots and took out the handheld pump and put ten pounds of air in each one. I pulled on my parka and gloves, strapped the ugly fur-lined hat's flaps under my chin, and then headed out of the bedroom.

"I was overheating before I even reached the door, only fifteen steps from my room. The sound that had awoken me from my dream-filled sleep had gone, and now nothing but silence filled the air; it was almost deafening. I exited the cabin and looked all around. The snow captured and then reflected the light coming from the open barn door and created multicolored sparkles; the landscape look like it was covered in diamonds. I turned around, went back into the cabin, and retrieved my camera.

"From the cabin porch, I took a half-dozen pictures without a flash. After turning the flash on, I focused on the tree line just past the barn and took a series of quick flash shots: click, click, click. The bright light from the flash attachment reflecting off the snow and penetrating the darkness looked like lightning, shooting through the forest and piercing the silence. It was almost as if I could hear the light as it made its way into the wilderness, disturbing its very fabric and changing it forever. But it didn't change it. It stayed unmoved and unspoiled. Maybe it was me who was disturbed. Maybe for an instant, it was the fabric of my mind and my perception that were changed forever.

"I'm not sure how long I stood there regaining my composure; it could have been a second or maybe an hour, but for the first time since I left the cabin, I noticed the cold. This cold was different from the cold that my mind was used to. It didn't cut into you, chilling you to the bone; it just sort of bit at your skin. There wasn't any breeze to move it through the layers of protection I had applied to myself. The air was dry, and it was like it wanted to snatch the moisture from my breath and disperse it into the world around me, to distribute my being into itself. I felt as if I was becoming entwined with the universe, no longer just in it but truly a part of it. I had a sense I was part of a dream, even though I knew I was completely awake. This feeling scared me a little and excited me even more. I wasn't sure if I was smiling, crying, or laughing out loud, but I must have been doing one of the three. Out of the corner of my eye, I glimpsed a shadow emerging from the light spilling out of the barn. It grew larger as the figure inside made its way to entrance. The shadow resembled a troll or maybe some type of mythical creature like the ones Miss Penny, my teacher and mentor from high school, taught about. It had a large head, and the body was broad and thick. The legs were extremely short and thin compared to its bulky upper body. It moved silently and smoothly as it approached the opening. I raised my camera and prepared to capture it as it revealed itself. I focused my lens, set the flash to high, and took a deep breath. As the figure emerged from the doorway, the shadow disappeared into the darkness, and the creature appeared in the flesh.

"I gasped and pushed the button on the camera. The flash lit up like a bomb going off, and I was blinded momentarily. I lowered the camera and blinked the flash image of the beast from my eyes just as it roared.

"Roared with laughter, that is. The laughter rose from the silence surrounding me and filled the forest. The trees swallowed the laughter as soon as it reached them and left me startled and embarrassed. Earl laughed again, and that made me laugh too.

"'Good morning, sleepy head,' he said. 'Glad you decided to join me.' The heat generated by the combination of fear, adrenaline, and embarrassment caused me to break out in a little sweat under my many layers of winter gear. It was replaced quickly by the dry cold that filled the air. I shivered and shook for a few seconds, and then I was dry and comfortable again. Once again, it was like the air itself sucked the moisture from me and dispersed it into the area all around, as if it was its own.

"I asked Earl what time it was, and he chuckled and replied, 'Time to get started.'

"As I thought about the time, I realized I hadn't seen a clock since I arrived here. No clock in the restaurant, no clock at the corner bank we passed on the way here, no clock in my room, or any room in the cabin at all. I looked at my watch and found it had stopped. It didn't look broken in any way, but the hands were dead still, even so. The only explanation I could come up with was the battery had died or maybe the watch was damaged somehow in the turbulence I experienced on the flight here; either way, it was stopped, and that was that. Even though I didn't know what time it was, I knew that I had slept, and now I was rested and ready to set out on the task at hand, getting my footage of the reindeer migration and producing my special for the news.

"Earl asked if I was hungry, and not surprisingly, I was starved. He lowered the long door to the barn, and we got into the old truck and headed back to the diner. We weaved our way back up the long driveway to the main road, and as we emerged, a light snow began to fall.

"Earl looked a bit worried about the snow, so I asked what was bothering him. He said, using a serious voice that worried me a little, that a storm was brewing, and it was going to be a monster. I figured it must be the one Rick had warned about before I left on this adventure.

"We arrived at the diner, and once again, it was nearly empty. The only other people there were Heather, our waitress from yesterday, and the two hunters.

"As we sat down, the hunters paid and left. They seemed to be in a big hurry, and Earl looked at them with a disapproving glare. I asked if he knew them, and he replied he knew the type.

"'Caribou hunters,' he grumbled, 'out to bag a trophy, a reindeer they can mount on their wall. Going to use the migration to trap them and pick them off without giving them a chance. We'll see how that goes for them,' he said under his breath.

"I asked what he meant, and he looked at me and gave me what he must have thought was a reassuring smile (it was anything but reassuring), and just said, 'Not to worry; things have a way of working themselves out.'

"We ordered and ate quickly. I paid and tipped Heather, and back in the truck we went. The snow was coming a bit harder now, and the roads were getting slick. Earl was in deep concentration while we made our way back to the cabin, so I just stayed quiet and watched the scenery pass by, taking the occasional picture to pass the time.

"We approached the entrance to Earl's cabin, and the lights from the truck lit up a small sign I hadn't see the first time we came here yesterday. It was in the shape of an arrow and was made of wood. The wood looked old and weathered, and printed on it in red letters in an old-looking script were the words 'The Great Northern Christmas Spirit & Tree Co.'"

* * *

I spilled my cocoa. Grandma stopped talking, and Dad went and got some paper towels to help me clean it up. Grandma asked if I was all right, but I couldn't say anything. I was in shock and just nodded my head. Dad continued to wipe up my mess, and Grandma resumed her story like nothing happened. I said I was sorry, but they both shrugged it off like it was a normal thing. Dad refilled my cup, but not quite to the top this time, and added eight new miniature marshmallows. I stirred it, and the aromatic steam rose and once again filled my nostrils and my mind, calming me. I raised the cup to my mouth and blew across the rising steam to cool the sweet nectar. As I did, I noticed that once again, the eight marshmallows had aligned themselves into four rows of two. I took a sip and thought about the sign Grandma described at Earl's cabin and wondered if it was the same one I had seen for the first time this year, the sign that led to the cabin in the woods where we picked up the Christmas tree on our way here. I decided it must be a replica of the one she spoke about and tried to just let it go.

I couldn't get it completely out of my head, so I pushed it back to the place of the mind that questions everything but allows you to get on with the things at hand. I refocused on Grandma's story but planned to ask about this sign later. For now, I just let it float back there in my mind, bouncing around and raising more questions as it did. I forced my thoughts back to Grandma and her story.

* * *

"We pulled back into the compound with the cabin and the barn and the tree line," she resumed. "It was still dark, and the snow was coming down at an even more intense rate. Earl parked the truck near the cabin and got out. He headed straight to the barn. It was clear that ever since we saw the hunters exit the diner, something had been bothering him. He didn't say so, but it was obvious to me something was different.

"I exited the truck and followed him. He opened the right side of the long doors in the front of the barn and then the left. There weren't any lights on in the barn, so when I got there, I peered in to see if I could tell what had made the noise that woke me up earlier. I could smell oil and gas, the sort of smells you encounter when you come across an old car that has been left to rot behind a garage.

"Earl went into the barn and disappeared into its darkness. I heard what sounded like a heavy-duty light switch click and then a humming sound. The hum was low at first but soon grew louder. I recognized it as the sound I heard when the security lights came on in the garage at the TV station. Soon there was a dim light coming from the ceiling of the barn. I couldn't see anything yet. There was another click of a switch and more humming. The light grew steadily, and I could almost make out a shape in the center of the barn.

"Earl walked up to me from the back of the dimly lit barn and said, 'We need to get going; the storm is increasing, and it will be light soon. If we don't leave now, we will miss our opportunity.'

"I asked where we were headed.

"Earl looked at me as if I was crazy and said, 'We are off to film the reindeer. Isn't that why you came here?'

"I laughed an embarrassing shy laugh and said I would go get my equipment and meet him at the truck. The light grew brighter in the barn. Earl looked me straight in the eye and said that we wouldn't need the truck for this part of the trip. He turned his gaze to the center of the barn, and as I turned my head to follow his gaze, I froze.

"'No way!' I yelled. 'You've got to be kidding. You can't be serious. Does that thing even work?'

"The thing I was talking about was an old airplane. When I say airplane, what I really mean is a large metal box with two engines and two propellers attached to those engines. The two engines were attached to two protrusions out the sides of the metal box. At the rear of the metal box was what some people might call a tail; I'm not one of those people. This tail thing sat at the complete end of the metal box and had wings sticking out of the sides about halfway up. The front of the plane, where the cockpit was, had a short windshield that wrapped around the sides. There were ski things where the wheels should have been, which made sense if we planned to take off and land in the snow, but I was hoping that wasn't going to be the case. Over the wings were three sets of windows. The front windows were much larger than the rear. Behind the wing on the left side of the plane was a door that opened outward and down and doubled as the stairs. The door was open, and the dim lights in the barn gave me a glimpse of things stacked in the plane. They looked to be boxes with some red writing on the sides. Under the cockpit area was painted in deep red old script, the name 'The Great Northern Christmas Spirit & Tree Co.' and above the windshield where it wrapped around on the pilot side, a name was printed in the same red script. It was small, and the lights weren't quite up to full power yet, so I couldn't make out what is said. I moved closer and read it. I looked over at Earl, and he just smiled. You guessed it: 'Earl' was what it said. I wasn't filled with much confidence at this point and decided that if I made it home, I was going to have a bit of a chat with Crystal, my travel agent."

Chapter 15

"Earl told me we needed to leave now if we were going to get any shots of the reindeer," Grandma continued, "so I headed into the cabin and collected my equipment. I once again heard the noise that had waken me up and realized it was the plane. The engines cranked up one at a time. The noise grew louder and louder, and as I exited the cabin, the plane emerged from its hiding place. It glided across the snow on those skis where the wheels should have been. I was surprised at how graceful it moved and even more shocked at how big it turned out to be. It was what I would call a cargo plane. It appeared more suited for transporting goods, not people, and I would soon experience the difference firsthand.

"I could see Earl in the pilot's seat, checking gauges and flipping switches. He was preparing for our trip and looked like he actually knew what he was doing.

"As I approached the plane, the engines slowed to an idle and the plane stopped gliding along the snow. Earl got up from his seat, and I saw through the side windows as he made his way to the back of the plane. The door behind the wing popped open again and settled onto the snow. Earl came down the steps and grabbed my camera bag. He motioned for me to follow him aboard, and I climbed the four steps up into the plane, ducking my head as I went through the opening. It was still cold inside the plane and pretty dark too.

"Earl sat my bag down against the wall that led into the cockpit, right behind where his seat was. He pointed to a seat across the aisle from my bag. It was about forty inches wide and was topped with a pad about four inches thick. The pad was made of brown faded leather. The sides of the seat had thin metal armrests, each one topped with the same leather. The back of the seat was short and would only come up midway on my back. It looked more like a bench than a chair and didn't give me the impression it was going to be very comfortable to ride in. One thing that helped ease my mind a little was it had a seat belt, and it looked like it worked. I guess looks can be deceiving.

"I sat down. I was right about the comfort of the seat but wrong about the seat belt.

"The seat was like sitting on a worn-out kitchen chair. The pad was thick, but it was all broken down like an old pillow. Once I sat down, it crushed under my rear and bunched up and was lumpy. I wiggled around and tried to make it form to my imprint, but that just made it worse. I decided to tough it out. I guess it was made more for function than comfort. The seat belt was just two straps of frayed leather with tarnished silver buckles attached to the ends. The buckles clicked together just fine, but only tightened to within five inches of my waist, even though I was wearing my thick parka and had my ski pants on. The frays of the leather kept the belts from getting any tighter. My guess was this seat was made for someone much larger around the waist than me. No matter what the cause or who normally sat here, I was hoping this trip was going to be smooth and quick.

"Earl walked past me and chuckled a little as he watched me getting settled in. He closed the door and latched it. He did a double-check of the cargo stored throughout the plane.

"I barely noticed the cargo when I got in and seated myself, but all around the plane were boxes strapped down. Some of them were red, but most of them were green. They were tied shut with ribbons. They looked like they were really old and had been used over and over again. I couldn't tell what was in them, but each one had a series of letters on the outside, just under the now-familiar red script that said 'The Great Northern Christmas Spirit & Tree Co.' The letters must have been some sort of filing system. The red boxes I could see from my seat had the letters A–K on one box and L–Q on another, and the last one was R–Z. The same thing was on the green boxes, but the ones I could see had

The Legend of Stormy and the Great Northern Christmas Spirit & Tree Company

A–D and E–H. Whatever was in the green boxes, there was certainly more of those per letter than the red ones.

"As Earl passed back through the cabin, he paused next to me. He looked me straight in the eyes, smiled, and asked if I was comfy. He knew better, but that was just his sense of humor. He then slid my equipment bag across the aisle to me and told me the ride might be a little rougher than I was used to. He said I might want to be prepared to film right away because there were a lot of beautiful and amazing things to see all along our upcoming trip. He entered the cockpit, sat down in the pilot's seat, and strapped in.

"I grabbed my bag, took out my still camera, and hung it around my neck, like I had done a hundred times before. I took out the video camera and three batteries. I snapped in the first battery and put the other two into the left pocket of my parka. I grabbed a recording tape from the bag and loaded the tape, closed the tape door, and turned the machine on. Looking through the eyepiece, I set the focus to auto, pointed the lens out the window, and hit the Record button. It was dark out, but I could still see the trees and the edge of the barn through the eyepiece, and I knew if I could see it, then so could the camera. I realized the snow was coming down even harder now and thought to myself it would look beautiful in my story, but what I should have been thinking is maybe this little plane shouldn't be getting ready to take off, with me in it, during what was building up to be a pretty good snowstorm. It may have been my desire to get this story or the opportunity to get my name on the news, or maybe, even though I had only known Earl a very short time, I felt safe with him and trusted he would protect me, but whatever it was, I was ready for my next adventure."

77

Chapter 16

"Earl turned to me and gave me a big smile and a not-so-reassuring thumbs-up. He pushed the throttle levers forward. The engines roared, and we started to move. It was as if someone was behind us, giving us a shove. We slid forward about four feet and stopped. Earl gave the throttle another little push, and again we started to move. At this point, it occurred to me all I had seen around me were trees and the cabin and barn. The driveway was narrow and winding, and the plane was way too big to get through there, so how was Earl going to get this plane in the air without a runway? My trust took a major dip.

"We swung to the right, and the wing on my side of the plane was running down the side of the barn past the big doors. The lights from the plane shown into the trees in front of us, and they were getting closer by the second. I was sure we would hit them any time now. Earl looked calm to me, but maybe he was just crazy. He reached for the throttles again, and I could feel the heat build in my parka. He pulled one throttle back, and the plane swung 90 degrees to the right; the wing slid around the corner of the barn, and Earl pushed the throttle back forward, and there it was, the opening, the clearing, the runway.

"I took a breath and lowered my fur-lined hood off my head. I raised the video camera and pointed it out the front windshield. Earl yelled, 'Hang on,' and pushed the throttles full forward. The engines roared, and the plane lunged forward. The nose lowered, and we continued to glide across the snow. As we picked up speed, we bounced and banged on the skis. I could see the tree line fast approaching through

The Legend of Stormy and the Great Northern Christmas Spirit & Tree Company

the camera's eyepiece at the other end of the clearing; the snow was beginning to pile up on the windshield. Visibility was decreasing, and we were running out of room. I panned the camera to the left, and Earl bent forward and flipped a switch. The wiper pulled itself from its hiding place and flipped the snow off the window, just in time for me to see tops of the trees slide below the plane. We were up and flying, and I never even felt the liftoff. I hoped this looked as crazy and scary on the video as it did in my mind.

"After we were safely in the air and Earl had things under control, he turned and handed me a set of headphones with a flexible mike attached to the right ear muff. I put them on, and the engine noise was almost completely blocked out. The cord ran to the front of the plane on the copilot's side and was plugged into a socket on the floor.

"I heard Earl say the mike is voice-activated. He said I would have to say, 'Check,' first and then speak so it would activate the mike before I started my conversation. I smiled and yelled, 'Check, I can hear you loud and clear.' Earl laughed and said, 'I hear you loud and clear too. You don't have to yell into the mike; they are very sensitive. Over.' I said in a normal voice, 'Check, over what?' 'Sorry,' he said, 'you say, "Over," when you're done speaking so the other person knows that they can respond, over.' 'Copy that, over,' and once again, I heard him laugh. His laugh calmed me somehow. It was warm and honest and made me feel like we were old friends.

"The plane continued to climb, and after ten minutes or so, the snow began to taper off. I took my camera and snapped a few more pictures. Some were of the snow-covered evergreens, which seemed to stretch out across the land forever. I also took photos of the mountains that breached the sky, and I even took one or two of Earl as he flew the plane. I let the still camera hang down around my neck, picked up the video camera, and shot some more scenery. It was starting to get brighter outside, and through the eyepiece, I was able to see things much clearer than just looking out the window. The zoom really pulled things in closer. I caught three moose trotting together. They looked up at us as if on cue. I guess the plane's engines caught their attention, but they seemed more curious than startled.

"I asked Earl how long until we saw the reindeer; he looked back and said, 'It's not far, really; less than forty minutes, over.'

"I nodded, and he turned back to the front. I continued videotaping. The snow was coming down much lighter and made the whole background sparkle again, like diamonds floating in the air. The time passed slowly. It grew lighter and lighter, and in the distance, I could see an eerie glow on the horizon. I videotaped it for a few minutes and then switched to the still camera and shot several more pictures. We were headed straight toward the glow, and it moved in waves of many colors. Earl must have been looking at it too because his voice filled the quiet in my head with the words 'Aurora borealis, the northern lights, as they are known; magnificent, isn't it?'

"Magnificent didn't even begin to describe it. If a picture is worth a thousand words, then the video I was taking would surely be a best-selling novel. It hypnotized me and took all the concentration I could muster just to stay focused on the job at hand. I felt I could live in this moment forever.

"We continued flying for another twenty minutes or so; I couldn't really be sure because my watch was still not working, and there wasn't anything that was normal like the sun to judge the time by. I still wasn't sure what time it was. It could have been eight o'clock in the morning or eight o'clock at night. We appeared to be getting closer to the northern lights, and it was becoming brighter, even though the sun was still not visible. I let myself believe it was sometime in the morning so I could keep a sense of reality.

"Earl's voice once again broke the silence; he said, 'Better get ready; we are almost there, over.'

"I checked the battery level on my video recorder. The level was less than 50 percent, so rather than risk missing any of the shots of reindeer, I dug into the pocket of my parka and took out a fresh battery and a new tape. After I replaced them, I took a minute of video to be sure everything was working correctly. Feeling confident I was ready, I scanned the area for reindeer, but all I could see were the northern lights overwhelming the entire landscape. They seemed to go on forever and reached all the way to the stars.

"Earl swung the plane to the right; the wing dipped down, and I could see a lake below my window. I put the eyepiece to my eye and hit Record. As I was scanning the area, I caught a glimpse of three animals at the right edge of the lake and zoomed in. As the focus adjusted, I could see they were polar bears and I knew from my research we must be in the artic region because that is the only area polar bears are found in Alaska. They looked as if they were fishing or something; all I could think of was, *This is going to be some amazing bonus footage for my piece.*

"As we passed over the lake, the plane leveled out, and we started to descend slowly. I kept the recording going, and then Earl said, 'We are going to take a large loop to the left, and when we are aligned with the northern lights on our right, we should have a great view of the reindeer. They migrate in a line with the oldest male of each family leading the younger ones and the oldest female trailing the family. This process continues as each family follows the others from beginning to end, over.'

"I asked why this was, and Earl said that was how the reindeer protected themselves from predators and danger. He also said it helped keep the younger ones from getting separated from the rest of the group. I responded, 'Check, copy that, over.' I liked the whole headphone language thing. It made me feel important somehow.

"The plane leveled off once again with the northern lights directly out my window and very close. They appeared to form a solid wall of colors: greens and blues mixed with shades of red. The wall itself moved in waves, silent waves of vibrant colors that shone for miles. The view overwhelmed my senses. I hit the Record button and tried to capture its beauty and power. Trust me, even Miss Penny never prepared me for this.

"As we continued, Earl held the plane steady. We were only about two or three thousand feet in the air but seemed like we were in outer space. I remember thinking I couldn't see anything on the other side of the lights. I knew there must be trees and mountains and snow, but none of it was visible through the glimmering brilliance of the lights. It was like we were on the edge of the earth, and this wall of lights was the only thing keeping us from disappearing into the abyss.

"Then almost out of nowhere, I saw through the camera's eyepiece a dark line approaching. I slowly zoomed in and could make out figures moving slowly towards us; we were moving toward them. Earl's voice once again filled my ears: 'There they are,' he said. 'Do you see them? Over.'

"'Check,' I replied. 'Copy that. I'm taping them now. How close will we get to them? Over.'

"He said we would fly right over them and then make another loop and come in for one more pass. After that, we needed to get back home before this storm cranked up.

"'Check,' I said. 'I'm getting some pretty good footage at this angle, over.'

"And I was getting good footage. I would say it was great footage. The line of reindeer was literally miles long and with the northern lights as a backdrop, the shot was amazing. The reindeer cast a shadow on the pure white snow, and the colors of the lights dancing off of them and onto the snow made them appear to be moving in slow motion. This was better than I imagined. Better than I hoped for."

Chapter 17

❦

Grandma continued, "We went on for another two or three minutes like this, with the video camera capturing everything perfectly. I zoomed in as close as the focus would allow. It was good enough for me to see the antlers and the faces of the deer. They were beautiful and proud-looking animals. They were lined up just as Earl had said. The lead reindeer in each group was a large male, and he was followed by several smaller deer and then an older-looking female at the end. There were hundreds of these groups marching like a caravan of nomads, searching for their next place to rest. We came near the end of the line, and Earl started his loop around.

"When we were lined up with the northern lights again, this time on our left, Earl hugged the lights much closer than before so I could keep the reindeer in my window's view. With this angle, the colorful, waving lights illuminated the deer themselves, and they looked as if they were dancing and not just walking. The lights made them look like cartoon figures from one of the Saturday morning shows I used to watch as a very young child. I caught focus of a small family, just an older large male and a smaller and younger male followed by an older female. This was the only group with just one young reindeer in it, and I figured it was a young family just starting out. As I was filming this young family, something up ahead of them caught my eye in the lens. It must have caught Earl's attention too because the plane began to pick up speed. I saw a flash and then another. The line of reindeer stopped their movement. I pointed the camera to where I saw the flash, and two figures came into view, men. They were just off the trail the reindeer were on. There was another flash. Guns, hunters, the men from the diner. They were hunting the reindeer. The deer just stood there, unsure of what was happening. I panned the camera down the line of reindeer and found the young family I was filming before and focused on them. The large male had taken a defensive stance in front of the young one, but it left the female out in the open. All the other groups were aligning in the same way. Clearly, this was not the type of predator they were used to encountering. I felt fear for the reindeer and anger toward the hunters. It was boiling up in me because there was nothing I could do for any of them. I kept filming the young family when Earl's voice rang out sharp and loud in my ears: 'ON!' he yelled.

"I wondered what he meant and was startled by its abrupt intrusion into my mind, but before I could reply, the plane took a violent turn to the right and seemed to drop from the sky. My worn seat belt with its tarnished buckles and the large gap around my waist did nothing to protect me from this extreme maneuver. I was raised from my seat and smashed against the window. My head crushed against the window frame, and even before I felt the pain, I could feel the warm flow of liquid running down the side of my face. I instinctively wiped the warm liquid with the sleeve of my white parka and its fur-lined cuffs, but all I saw was red. Bright sickening red and I knew right then the warm red liquid was blood, my blood, and lots of it.

"I still had the video camera in my right hand, held there by the strap that steadied it, and I pointed it out the window and looked through the eyepiece. It was blurry, and at first, I thought it must have been damaged. That's when I realized the camera was all right; it was my vision that was blurry. My right eye was swelling shut. I strained with my left eye and just aimed the camera as best I could through the window at the reindeer and the hunters and the ground, which was coming up rapidly. We were crashing; I was sure of it. Were we hit by a blast from the hunters' guns? Was Earl hit? Had he lost control of the plane? Why wasn't he talking to me?

"That's when I noticed my headphones were missing. They must have been knocked off when my head hit the window. I looked over at Earl, and he was yelling something to me, but with the noise of the now-screaming engines and the pounding of my heart in my ears, I couldn't make out what he was saying. At least he was still in control of the plane. I took another look out the window with my one good eye and saw something I didn't expect: The reindeer were scattering. They kept in their smaller groups and darted right and left. Earl had used the plane to disperse the deer, so the hunters couldn't get an easy shot. The young family I had been filming was running wildly. I kept my camera pointed in their direction, even though I wasn't sure if I was filming them or the ground or just the wall of color that was the northern lights.

"The plane started to pull up, and we narrowly missed the top of the trees. As we climbed back into the sky, I locked my left arm under my seat belt and held on. 'Hold on.' That's what Earl must have been saying just before our abrupt flight pattern change. Hold on. It only came out as 'On' because in the excitement he must have forgotten to say, 'Check,' first.

"The reindeer were scattered all around at this point; the hunters' day was over. The snow was falling again, and Earl turned the wiper back on. The camera was getting heavy, and the last thing I could see clearly from my window was the young deer stopped and looking around, like he was lost. His parents were nowhere to be seen, and one of the hunters was raising his gun once more. Earl swung the plane in the young deer's direction and gunned the throttle. My heart pounded even harder, and I screamed, 'Run,' as loud as I could.

"The young deer leaped and ran, the gun flashed, and the deer disappeared into the wall of lights. With all of the noise and excitement and the loss of blood, I started to feel woozy. I feared I would soon pass out, and then we entered the wall ourselves. The plane lurched left and right and bucked up and down. From my window, I could see all the waves of color rushing by. I saw stars and what appeared to be flashes of lightning. I figured I was falling unconscious because one of the last things I thought I saw was that young reindeer, flying through the sky, looking frantically for something. The other thing I saw was one of those red boxes that had come loose and popped open. In it was a bunch of invoices or slips of paper. The one on top had my name on it and some notes written below. I couldn't make out what the notes said. And then there was nothing but darkness."

* * *

I looked into Grandma's eyes. She was no longer here in the living room with the tree and my dad and me. She was somewhere in Alaska, inside a plane with a guy named Earl, back in a time way before me, way before my dad. She was in her story, and so was I. I sipped my cocoa and listened on.

* * *

"I heard the plane's engines first," she continued. "They were steady and strong, and I knew we were no longer in any danger of crashing. As I opened my eyes, the sky looked different to me. It was brighter than before, but I still didn't see the sun, or the moon, for that matter. The brightness seemed to come from everywhere and nowhere at all. It was just there. I blinked a couple of times and tried to get my wits about me. Earl was still flying the plane. He looked back at me, and I could see an expression of relief on his face. He pointed to the floor and then to his headphones. I looked down, found my headphones, and put them on. I still had the camera strapped to my right hand, and it was still recording, so I pushed the Stop button and laid it on the seat next to me. The blood had stopped flowing from the wound on my head, and it was dry on the sleeve my parka. I was able to see out of both eyes but could tell that my right one was swollen. I was surprised to find I didn't feel any pain. With the headphones back in place, I heard the sweetest sound that I could remember. It was Earl's voice. All he said was, 'Sorry, over.' I started laughing and crying all at the same time, and he looked back and smiled at me.

"I continued to laugh and replied, 'Check, sorry? That's all you have to say to me, sorry? You ruined my coat and everything. What happened back there? How long was I out? Did the reindeer get away? Where are we? Over.'

"'All in due time,' he replied. 'First, we have to get this plane on the ground before the storm gets any worse, over.'"

Chapter 18

"The wipers were on and running full speed," Grandma said. "The snow was the heaviest I had seen it since leaving home. We were descending at a comfortable pace, and I now had full confidence in Earl's ability as a pilot and a guide. We were coming into the tree line, but I couldn't see a clearing yet. Out of the windshield, I saw what appeared to be a small town, but it was obscured because of the snow. It looked a lot different from North Pole, where the cabin was, but I figured Earl knew it well enough and was going to put the plane down there to avoid flying any longer in this weather.

"As we got closer, I could make out several homes and some businesses. There was one main road, and it was lined with stores, and then several small side streets with homes. I didn't see any vehicles moving around, but that didn't worry me much. What did worry me was I didn't see any airport or anything that looked like a landing strip. All I saw was the little town and the stores and the houses. We circled the town; I saw a few people walking around and what looked like reindeer roaming the streets, almost like they were sharing the roadways. We passed over the town, and on the outskirts, there was a large home with a barn, just like the one at Earl's cabin.

"Behind the barn was a clearing, and we headed straight for it. The snow was now almost blinding, but Earl banked the plane to the left and aligned us up with the snow-covered landing strip, and as smooth as it could have been, the plane crossed over the treetops and set down on the snow. The skis on the plane just slid across the snow, and we coasted to a stop. Earl spun the plane around and headed us back toward the barn and the large house. We stopped right in front of the barn, and the engine noise finally stopped, giving way to silence. I took my headphones off and unbuckled my seat belt; Earl was already out of his seat and straightening up the boxes that had dislodged during our eventful flight. I saw him glance my way as he closed up the red one with the papers in it that had my name on it. He seemed to be trying to see if I had noticed it, and I acted as if I hadn't.

"I collected my camera stuff and packed them away into their carrying bag. I kept the still camera around my neck, just in case I saw something interesting, but I was doubtful this little town had anything exciting to film. The falling snow covered the planes windows and the inside of the plane became dark. Earl started to open the door. He turned and gave me a very serious look and said, 'This place might seem a little strange, even weird at first, but you'll get used to it.' As soon as the door was open and my eyes adjusted to the light again, things took a turn to the weird side, and I mean full-blown weird."

* * *

For the first time since I spilled my cocoa, Grandma looked at me in a way that told me she was finally back in the room with us. She had a serious look in her eyes, and it kind of scared me. What she said next didn't fill me with much confidence this story was going to go the way I had expected.

She took a long draft from her cocoa, looked at my dad and back to me, and said, "The next part of my story is going to sound a little far-fetched. No, I take that back; the next part of this story is going to sound absolutely crazy, but please listen carefully and don't make any judgements till I'm done."

I nodded, but I wasn't so sure if I was ready for what was to come. So far, her story sounded like just that: a story. What was to come must be the whole reason for the story itself. Up to now, it was interesting, exciting even, but it didn't touch on any of the traditions. It didn't cover any of the adult secrets I hoped would propel me into that next stage of my life. I left my expectations dangle in the back of my mind and just tried to focus on the story. I trusted the storyteller completely. Grandma was always there for me, no matter what, and I was sure she was not going to let me down this time, so I just settled back, took another sip from my cup, and let her continue.

* * *

"As I said, things started to get weird as soon as the door of the plane opened," she continued. "The cold air entered along with wisps of snow. I heard voices outside the plane, and Earl was acting a little anxious. Based on the number of different voices, there must have been several people waiting outside the plane. Because the snow covered the windows, I wasn't able see anyone, but I could hear them. They must have known that we were coming because we were in the middle of nowhere and they were still there to meet us. Maybe when I blacked out, Earl radioed ahead for help.

"Earl came back to my seat. He looked at me very seriously and told me not to be scared, to try and stay calm and not freak out. I asked him why, and all he said was things were a little different here. How different, I wasn't prepared for, so I just got out of my seat, grabbed my camera bag, and followed Earl past the red and green boxes and out the door.

"As I exited the plane and carefully walked down the steps of the door, my eyes continued to adjust to the strange light that reflected off the deep snow, which covered everything surrounding us. The trees were covered with snow. The plane was covered with snow. The large barn, the one just like the barn back at Earl's cabin, was covered with snow. The next thing I noticed were the two carriages next to the plane. One looked like a regular carriage, the type you might see in Central Park in New York City, the type of carriage pulled by horses and occupied by couples taking a romantic ride, only this one had two reindeer hitched to it and skis where the wheels would have been, just like Earl's plane.

"The other one was more like a low-sided wagon. It also had reindeer hitched to it, but they were bigger than the two hitched to the carriage.

There was man standing next to the larger carriage. He looked to be the same age as Earl and had a similar build. He was wearing a blue parka with blue pants and red mittens. I looked around for more people, but he was the only one I saw. I could have sworn I had heard at least four or five voices before we exited the plane.

"The old man in the blue parka looked up at me and asked Earl who the girl was; that girl was me, but I hadn't been called a girl by anyone since I was in high school. Earl looked at me and laughed. He introduced me as Miss Jane and told me the old man was called Gary. I shook Gary's hand, well, his mitten.

"Gary looked me over and asked if I was okay. Then he looked back at Earl and said I needed medical attention.

"I had almost forgotten about smashing my head against the side of the plane before we passed through the northern lights. The blood still stained my white parka, but it had stopped flowing from the wound above my eye; the pain was pretty much gone, but the cut and lump were still there.

"Since Gary reminded me of the damage to my head, I started to get woozy again. It must have been showing because Earl and Gary both looked at me with concerned looks on their faces. Suddenly, I started hearing other voices. I couldn't tell where the voices were coming from, but I could hear them clear as could be. They seemed to be speaking to Earl and Gary and not me. They sounded concerned about my health and also about the heavy snow that was falling. Earl and Gary took me by the arms and helped me into the carriage, and Earl climbed in next to me. Gary assured Earl that he would take care of the plane and the boxes and would catch up with him later. The other voices chimed in; I looked around for who was speaking, but I could only see the reindeer."

* * *

Grandma looked at me and said, "I warned you this was going to start sounding crazy. Please keep an open mind because the real crazy hasn't even begun yet."

The Legend of Stormy and the Great Northern Christmas Spirit & Tree Company

I just nodded and let her continue.

* * *

"Earl sat next to me on my left and asked if I was okay. I nodded, and he called out to the reindeer, 'Off to Nick's, please,' and the carriage began to move. The reindeer pulled it with no effort at all.

"We left the barn and the plane behind us and headed into the woods. Just before the plane was out of sight, I turned and saw Gary loading the boxes from the plane onto the wagon, and then it was out of sight. There was a trail winding through the trees, and the reindeer maneuvered us through it without any guidance from Earl at all. I heard their bells jingle as they strode along. The sound of the bells reminded me of something from my youth. It was a Christmas-type sound, and riding through the forest of evergreens dusted with fresh snow, I started to feel like a child again.

"We emerged from the trees and onto what appeared to be some sort of a main street. We turned right, and I could see trails of smoke rising like pillars in the distance. On the left was a side street. It had a wooden sign at the corner that said St. Gary. The sign was painted in old script. The letters were red and slightly faded. I glanced down the side street and saw three log cabins. In the front of each home was a beautifully decorated evergreen. They had bulbs and ornaments hung all over them. There were bells on several of the branches. The bells were the same as the ones the reindeer wore, and as the breeze blew, I could hear them ringing softly. Their tune mixed with the ones from the two reindeer pulling our sleigh, and it was if they were answering each other. Most of the bulbs on the trees were blue, with the exception of a few silver and gold ones. As we continued toward the pillars of smoke, the road wound to the left in an arc and continued through the evergreens. Some distance up the road was another side street on the left. I looked down this street and saw more log homes. There were four of them, two on the right and two on the left. Each one had an evergreen out front. The two on the left were larger and taller than the two on the right. These trees were also decorated. The pattern of decoration was similar to the trees in front of the homes on St. Gary, with the main difference being that the majority of bulbs were pink. On the wooden sign at the end of this side street were the words, St Tina. I realized the pillars of smoke I was seeing were coming from the chimneys of these log homes.

"We continued along the road and came to a larger road on our left. This one was much different than the previous side streets we had passed. It had a much larger sign atop of a taller post. The sign was painted the same as the others, red paint and old script, but this one said 'St Nicolas.' We turned down this road, and the trees started to thin out.

"This road was wider and ran straight for a great distance. Off to the left was a large log home, much larger than the ones I saw before. It had several outbuildings. One looked like it was a garage. It had a single wide door in front and a smaller door to the side. There were two trails leading up to and disappearing under the larger door in the front. I figured those trails were made by ski runners like the ones on the sleigh we were riding in. I decided this must be the mode of transportation here, wherever here was.

"This property also had a large stable behind the main home. It looked like it could hold several animals like horses or maybe reindeer. I saw eight separate doors across the front of this structure. It looked like it was currently not occupied, and it was the same with the home out front. Both still had smoke coming from the chimneys but were otherwise dark. This home had three evergreens out front. The center one was about fifteen feet tall and the two on either side of it seven or eight feet tall. The center one was decorated in mostly red with some gold and silver. The other two were covered in all colors. They had more of the specialty ornaments and were full from top to bottom.

"The snow was coming down harder, and as we passed this home, I thought I heard Christmas carols being sung. I couldn't tell where they were coming from, but I saw the reindeer that were pulling the sleigh look up into the sky. Earl looked up too, so I followed his gaze. Through the falling snow, I saw something overhead in the distance crossing the sky from left to right. I couldn't make out what it was, but it seemed like the carols were coming from the object in the sky. I heard Earl say, 'Who's that?' and looked at him like, how would I know?

"This is when I figured out he wasn't talking to me. I guessed he was just talking to himself out loud, and he did it again. I heard other voices, two of them, and they seemed to be answering Earl. The first voice was low and sounded like an old man. I couldn't figure out where it was coming from, but it seemed to say, 'He came through with you.' The second voice was also a male voice but sounded much younger. It too replied to Earl's question, saying there were reported to be three in all who came through at the same time, but they became separated in the storm.

"Once again, I started feeling woozy. It was like I had hit my head all over again, only this time, the woozy came from inside my mind. I figured I was hallucinating because it seemed like the voices were coming from the reindeer themselves. This scared me even more because I wasn't even sure where we were, and if I was this injured, how would I get to a hospital? I started to panic. Earl looked at me and asked if I was all right. I shook my head, and for the first time, I saw some fear in Earl's eyes. I started crying, but Earl told me to relax and hang on. And then he said, 'Quick, get us to Doc Brian's.'

"The sleigh bolted forward. It felt lighter; I felt lighter. It felt like we were flying. I saw stars, and then everything went black."

Chapter 19

Grandma continued, "The first thing I remember before I opened my eyes was the smell. It was sweet and smooth. It made me think of being back at home on a cold winter's evening with my parents. It was chocolatey and warm; it smelled like cocoa. I opened my eyes, half-expecting to see my mom standing over me with a steaming mug in one hand and a plate of sugar cookies in the other.

"I blinked and looked up at the ceiling; it was made of wooden beams all wedged together. I had no idea where I was. The last thing I remembered was riding on the sleigh with Earl, the voices, and the feeling of weightlessness. I didn't know how long I was out or where Earl was. I wasn't sure if I was still sleeping; was this all some sort of dream?

"I looked around and saw I was in a bedroom; there was a window to my left, and the door was directly in front of me. On my right was a nightstand with a large mug, steam rising from it, and next to the mug was a plate of sugar cookies. That is what I must have smelled as I awoke.

"I sat up, maybe too fast because I felt a little dizzy. Before I could regain my focus, there was a knock at the door, and it opened slowly. A woman who was in her thirties with shoulder-length brown hair entered and smiled at me; she had a small gap between her top front two teeth and a small nose. Even though I had never met her before, she seemed caring, and her voice was calm and pleasant.

"'Good to see you finally awake, Miss Jane,' she said. 'You sure gave

The Legend of Stormy and the Great Northern Christmas Spirit & Tree Company

us quite a start. My name is Kelly, and if you need or want anything at all, please don't hesitate to ask. Doc Brian will be with you shortly.'

"I asked where I was and where Earl was. 'Is this the hospital?' I asked. Kelly let out a little laugh and said, 'There is no hospital up here, at least not like you're used to. This is Doc Brian's home. He is the only medicine man for a long ways. Doc Brian is more a veterinarian than a medical doctor, but he's taken care of both the animals and the people here for as long as I can remember and is very good at it.'

"As she was speaking, I noticed I was dressed in a full-length nightgown, and my head was wrapped in a gauze bandage. Kelly picked up the mug from the nightstand and handed it to me. She suggested that I take a few sips and maybe eat a cookie or two to help me regain my strength. I was hungry and very thirsty, so I took the mug and raised it to my mouth. I blew the steam off and saw some miniature marshmallows floating on top. I took a sip; it was amazing. It was smooth and warm and sweet. I felt better almost immediately and was starving, so I grabbed a cookie off the plate. It was baked in the shape of a Christmas tree and was still warm. It had thick red and green frosting with sprinkles on top and was even better than my mom's. I finished it in three bites. I sipped some more cocoa and ate another cookie and felt almost normal again."

* * *

When Grandma talked about eating the cookies, I found myself craving some more cookies myself. I reached over and grabbed two from the plate; after the first bite, I couldn't imagine the ones she described were better than these. I took another bite and then a sip of cocoa and listened on.

* * *

"I asked Kelly if there was a bathroom I could use, and she took my hand and helped me up. I was surprised at how weak I felt. My legs were wobbly, and my head began to spin a little. She put her arm under my arm and guided me out of the room and down a long hallway. Halfway down the hallway on the left was another room. I peered into it as we passed and saw a desk and chair. The desk was covered with papers; an oil lamp hung from the ceiling, burning dimly, and a small wood stove was in the corner near a window. The glow from the wood stove was almost as bright as the oil lamp. I assumed this was Doc Brian's office, but I still hadn't met him, and he wasn't in there. Just past the office and on the right was another door. The end of the hall opened up into a large room with a window; I could see it was still snowing outside and even harder yet. The door to the right turned out to be the bathroom. Kelly opened the door, and I went inside and shut it behind me. The bathroom was lit with another oil lamp. I fumbled for the wick adjuster and turned it up. The room slowly became brighter.

"My eyes took a few seconds to adjust, but when they did, I saw a rather large sink with a mirror above it. The sink had a pump to make the water come out, and after I moved the lever up and down a few times, water started to flow. I splashed the water on my face and found it to be extremely cold and refreshing. I looked up into the mirror and saw, for the first time, how much damage the window had done to my head. My right eye was swollen and black and blue. There was a bandage above it and a wrap that went all the way around my head. Some blood had seeped through the bandage, but it had dried. Kelly called through the door to make sure I was okay, and I assured her I was. I finished my business, and she led me back to the bedroom where I had first woken up.

"Earl was in the room when we returned with another man, who turned out to be Doc Brian. Kelly helped me back to the bed. I sat down, and Doc Brian asked if he could take a look at my wound. I nodded, and he began to take the wrap and bandage off while Kelly assisted.

"Doc Brian was a fairly handsome man of about forty-five. He was in good shape for his age and stood around six feet tall. His skin was dark, and he had a scar on his right cheek, making him look quite rugged. His hair was dark, and the temples were sprinkled with gray, giving him a look of intelligence and experience.

"As Doc Brian removed the wrap and the bandage, Earl was looking at me with a smile, but his eyes betrayed him. I could see the concern, almost fear, in them. Doc Brian cleaned the wound with a solution that smelled sweet but stung like fire.

"I asked how bad it was. Earl seemed as concerned as me, even though his smile never faded.

"'Well,' Doc Brian replied, 'the truth is, the cut is pretty deep, and I had to put several stiches in it to stop the bleeding. Unfortunately, they will leave a nasty scar, but you should heal just fine otherwise. You lost a lot of blood, and that's what's making you dizzy and weak. You'll need at least another day of rest and maybe some more cocoa and cookies. Kelly has offered to look after you and change your bandage; I will look in on you from time to time to make sure you're doing okay. For now, try to get comfortable and rest. I've got another patient to attend to right now, but I'll be back later.'

"Earl gave me a little hug and whispered, 'I'm sorry,' which made me feel better and a little sad all at once. I gave him a smile and a nod to let him know I didn't blame him; after all, he had always been kind to me and made me feel welcome. He was like an uncle to me, even though I had only known him a short time.

"The two of them left the room, and Kelly helped me get settled back into the bed. I thanked her, and as she was left the room, I asked her how long I had been out. Her response made me uncomfortable. She said I was brought here late yesterday and that it was now midday.

"This meant that before I was going to be any better, I'd have to be here three more days. My trip back home was scheduled for tomorrow; I wasn't even sure where I was right now or when we'd get back to Earl's house. If I didn't make my flight, I'd be late getting back to the station, and my story wouldn't have time to air, and this trip would be all for nothing. This was the last thing I remember thinking about as I slipped off to sleep.

"Once again, dreams filled my sleep. This was the second time I remember dreaming in years. The dreams were fun and safe and a little crazy. I dreamed of the Christmases of my childhood. It was beautiful. I saw my mom and dad putting up the tree. I smelled the sweet pine scent that filled the house. We sang carols and had cookies and cocoa, but the cocoa tasted like the cocoa I had here and at Earl's house, not like the cocoa we drank at home. I dreamed of waking up on Christmas morning and seeing the presents under the tree. I rushed over and began to open them. I got a tricycle and a new dress. There were a pair of shoes, and a hat I loved and wore till it fell apart. There were coloring books and a new box of crayons, a big box with forty-eight crayons in it, and best of all, I got a doll. Not just any doll, but the doll that I asked Santa for when I went to the big department store downtown two weeks before Christmas. I was older in the next dream. I guess I was about your age, Brandi."

* * *

This shocked me out of the trance I was in, listening to Grandma's story. This was the first time since she started talking that she actually acknowledged telling me a story and not just recalling the past out loud. It was right then I noticed it. It was like when you see something all your life, and it just seems normal and belongs there, so you never question it, and someone points it out, and you recognize it for what it truly is, and it sticks out like a sore thumb. It was just above her right eye and left a small gap on the end of her eyebrow. *It* was a scar, a scar that had shrunk and smoothed and healed over time, but a scar is what it was.

I know it's a scar because I have one similar to it above my left eye. I got my scar when I was five. It happened while I was learning to ride my first two-wheel bicycle. My dad took great caution and showed extreme care in teaching me how to ride. He would run behind me, holding onto the seat so I wouldn't fall, and shout, "Peddle, peddle, peddle," so I could keep going. When he finally decided I was ready to ride solo, he let go of the seat. I rode all by myself, but he neglected to give me one important bit of information. He forgot to show me how to stop.

He ran behind me, shouting, "Peddle, peddle, peddle," and I kept peddling, and then I turned into the neighbor's driveway and up their sidewalk and right up to the new screen door they had just finished installing, and right through it. The lip of the door hit my forehead,

The Legend of Stormy and the Great Northern Christmas Spirit & Tree Company

and the bike stopped on its own, and the blood flowed freely. Off to the hospital and ten stiches later, I had a scar.

I reached up and rubbed my old scar and looked once more at Grandma's scar, the one I had just seen for the first time, and this caused me to zero in on her every word from now on.

* * *

"The next dream," she continued, "was a little stranger. I was in my middle school choir, and we were halfway through the annual Christmas concert. The program was running smoothly, but then our voices began to echo back at us from above the auditorium. The entire choir looked up toward the ceiling, and it was sparkling, like snowflakes falling through streetlights on a calm winter's night. As we continued to sing, I thought I saw something flying across that sparkling ceiling. I strained my dream eyes to see if I could make out what it was, but I couldn't. Whatever the object moving across the ceiling above us was, it was singing along with us, and I had a feeling it had a greater purpose for being there, but I couldn't understand what it was. The auditorium went dark, and the dream was over.

"I opened my eyes, and Kelly was sitting in a chair next to my bed. There was another mug of cocoa on the nightstand and another plate of cookies. I felt completely rested this time and sat up without any help at all. I wasn't the slightest bit dizzy, and my eyes could focus perfectly.

"Kelly smiled and asked if I was hungry, and I nodded. She held out the plate of cookies, and I snapped up two of them and picked up the mug of cocoa. I blew the steam off the top and took a good long draft; there were eight miniature marshmallows, aligned in four rows of two. I felt stronger than I had since I first hit my head in the plane. I wasn't perfect, but I felt pretty good. At the foot of the bed, I saw my clothes: my ski pants, my long johns, and my parka. My hat and gloves were there, and on the floor were my boots. My parka was clean, and all the blood was gone.

"I asked Kelly if I could use the bathroom again, and this time, I was able to go without any help at all. I pumped the water spout and splashed my face again. I looked pretty good in the mirror, and my head no longer had the wrap around it. There was still a large bandage over my right eye but the swelling had gone down and the bandage was clean, no more seeping blood.

"I returned to the room, and the curtains were now open. I couldn't tell if it was morning, noon, or night because it was dark out, except for the eerie glow of the northern lights. The snow was coming down strong, and I knew I would not be leaving this place soon.

"Kelly left the room, and I changed out of the nightgown and back into my winter clothes. I made the bed, folded the gown, and placed it on the chair Kelly had been sitting on. I grabbed the last cookie off the plate. It was the largest one so far and was in the shape of a reindeer. It was covered in chocolate frosting and decorated with silver and green sprinkles around the neck; it look like a set of jingle bells. Even though it was pretty, I finished it off in three tasty bites and drained the final drops of cocoa from the mug. I pulled on my boots, stuffed my gloves and hat into the pockets of my parka, and took the plate and mug with me into the hall.

"I found Kelly in the living room with Earl. They both turned to me, and Earl smiled, but it wasn't a real comforting smile. His eyes showed worry and stress, and we both spoke the same words at the same time: 'Are you all right?'

"I answered first. I told him I was feeling much better and thanked Kelly for helping me. I asked him again if he was all right.

"Earl asked me if I was ready to get out of this cabin, and I nodded. Kelly said goodbye, and we left."

Chapter 20

❦

"We left Doc Brian's place through the front door," Grandma said, "and headed down the steps off the porch. The same two reindeer were hitched to the same sleigh we used before. They looked over at me, and at first, I thought it was coincidence, but they both winked and nodded to me. I don't know why, but I nodded and winked back at them and thought I heard them give me a little chuckle. We climbed aboard the sleigh, and Earl told the reindeer to head back to Nick's, and off we went.

"We pulled out of Doc Brian's driveway and passed three more log homes on his street. Each one had a decorated evergreen out front. Each of these trees was decorated in mostly purple but had some silver and gold mixed in. I was detecting a pattern and decided it was time to start asking Earl some questions. He must have been reading my mind because he looked at me and said, 'I'll bet there are a few things you would like to know.'

"As we approached the end of the street, there was a wooden sign in the shape of an arrow with the words 'St Earl' written on it. The two reindeer turned the sleigh left, and we were back on the same main road we started on before I blacked out the first time. I began to hear the Christmas carols again. We all looked up, and this time, I saw it. The object flying through the air was without a doubt a reindeer. Yes, you heard me right: a flying reindeer. And not just any flying reindeer; this flying reindeer was singing Christmas carols. My first thought was I was still back in Doc Brian's home, still asleep and dreaming, but Earl

Thomas L Jaegly

nudged me, pointed at the flying reindeer, and said, 'He's new here. He came through with us when we entered the lights. No one is sure why he does it, but he flies around all day and night, just singing Christmas carols. He crisscrosses the sky for some unknown reason. No one has had a chance to speak with him, but he'll have to land sometime to rest."

"I heard the other voices again and feared I was losing my mind. The first voice said, 'I remember when I first came through. The freedom of flight was so new and powerful, I stayed up for a whole day myself.'

"It was at this point I realized the voices I was hearing were coming from the reindeer pulling the sleigh. The other one said, 'I was born here and was flying as soon as I was walking, so it was just natural to me.'

"I looked at Earl, and his regular smile was back. He turned to me and said, 'I told you things were going to get weird. Yes, the reindeer here fly, and yes, they talk.'

"All I could say was, 'How is that even possible?' The older reindeer turned back at me and said, in his deep voice, 'I asked the exact same thing the first time Earl and Nick showed up here. Who knew people could talk.'

* * *

That's when I did it. I told Grandma to stop. It wasn't just the word *Stop*; it was the tone I used with that word that caused the silence, the silence that made me feel as if I had crossed a line, a line I never really knew existed in the first place. But it did exist, and when I found myself on the other side of it, I didn't know what to do next or how to get back.

Dad looked at me. Grandma looked at me. If I had a mirror and looked at myself, I wonder who I'd have seen.

Grandma broke the silence and said, "I understand what you must think, and if you want me to stop, then I will respect your wishes."

This was the first time in my life that I was given an adult choice in what was going on around me. To be truthful, it didn't feel all that great, and it wasn't the way I thought it would be. I wasn't sure what the adult answer should be so, I just said I was sorry and asked her to please continue. She picked up where she left off, and after a long drink of my cocoa, I was right back there with her.

* * *

"Earl was the next to speak," she continued as if nothing had happened, "and then the whole thing was out in the open.

"He said, 'This is a special place. Things here are not as they are in the rest of the world. We live to take care of each other and protect each other.'

"'Okay,' I said, 'where exactly are we? Is this the North Pole, or are we in Christmastown?'

"Earl laughed a hearty laugh. It was a belly laugh that made his cheeks puff out a little and grow a little red and rosy. The reindeer laughed too, and the sleigh jerked ahead; I almost fell out, but I was serious. I wanted to know what this place was. Earl could see I was serious and even a little afraid, so he spoke right up.

"He started by saying, 'No, this isn't the North Pole; the North Pole is quite some distance from here. We are south of the North Pole and near what is called the Magnetic North. It is where your compass points when it points north. That is what keeps us hidden from the rest of the world; well, that and the aurora borealis that surrounds us. The magnetism and the northern lights create a natural barrier to travelers who come too close. The lights keep us hidden, and the magnetism throws off the navigation systems, so most everyone goes around us without even noticing us. Nick and I stumbled on this place by accident. Now as for Christmastown, it sure would be a good description, but I don't think such a place really exists. Christmastown is a legend created by people long ago to explain some of the special things that happen on Christmas Eve and Christmas Day, things like flying reindeer, sleighs filled with toys for good girls and boys all across the world, and such. But that is not where we are. We are at what we call the Great Northern Christmas Spirit & Tree Co. This place is what is known as a company town. Everyone here has a special talent or gift that contributes to the community and the company, and these talents are shared equally and freely so everyone lives a fulfilling life. I'm probably not the best one to explain all this to you, and besides, I have to meet with a group of the company's leaders about a situation that has arisen, so I'm going to have Eric and Kevin drop me off at my brother Nick's place and then take you to our friend Tina's."

"The older reindeer said his name was Eric. The other one said, 'I'm Kevin, and you can tell us apart because I'm the good-looking one.' Eric snorted a little and said, 'Whatever; at least I'm the strong one.'

"Earl told them to cool off. He let them know this wasn't the time to have this discussion again. We turned back onto St Nicolas and pulled in front of the home with the three evergreens in front. Several other reindeer were standing outside, along with a few more sleighs. This time, there were lights burning in the windows of the home and footprints in the snow leading up the porch to the front door. Earl got out of the sleigh, waved goodbye, and headed up the steps toward the door.

"Eric and Kevin nodded to the other reindeer, and we were off once again. We turned right out of the driveway onto St Nicolas and continued till we came to a circle with a decorated evergreen in the center of it. The decorations on this tree were very similar to the ones on the smaller trees at Nick's place. They were all different colors. The bulbs were large and small and in all different shapes. As we made our way around the circle, I noticed the tree was decorated evenly all the way around.

"Right then, the younger reindeer, Kevin, said, 'Here he comes again, here comes Stormy.' I could hear the carol he was singing before I spotted him, but it was him all right. I asked Kevin why he called him Stormy, and Eric replied, 'Well, we don't know his name, and we have to call him something, so one time when he was flying by, Kevin yelled out, "Hey, Stormy" because he came through during the storm we are having, and he looked down at us, so it just stuck.'

"I asked him what he was doing up there, and Kevin said he thinks he's looking for something or maybe someone.

"Eric replied in a sarcastic tone, 'Duh, ya think? I just wonder why he sings all the time.' Kevin seemed like he wanted to reply, but I guess he couldn't think of a good comeback, so he just shook his head and snorted.

"We passed the first quarter of the roundabout, and the road on our right had a sign that read 'St Earl E.' We came around to the other side of the roundabout, and the sign there read 'St Nicolas N.' We continued on around until we arrived at St Earl W and made another right. We traveled past several side streets. Each one had a wooden sign painted in the same old script with red letters, and they all said 'St this name' and 'St that name.' This confused me, but I decided at some point I would ask about this phenomenon. All of the side streets had log homes on them; each home had an evergreen out front decorated with colored bulbs, and on each street, the bulbs were all the same color but different from the next street. This was another thing I wanted to ask about. I decided I should take some pictures and realized my camera was missing. I knew I had it when I left the plane but didn't remember seeing it since. Another question, I guess.

"We came to the end of St Earl W and went left on the outer circle road and back toward the way we started. This confused me because it would have been much shorter and quicker if we had just turned left in the first place when we were leaving Nick's place, so I asked Eric why he went this way; he said the circle streets only ran one way, counterclockwise. This didn't make any sense to me, either, because the road was plenty wide for sleighs traveling in different directions to pass each other, but I just let it go.

"We turned left onto the next side street; its sign read 'St Tina.' We traveled a short ways to a small log home that looked more like a cottage. It had a perfectly decorated evergreen out front with all pink bulbs on it and several handmade ornaments along with jingle bells and some fancy ribbons.

"Eric told me this was Tina's home, and she would be my guide going forward. I climbed down from the sleigh and headed for the house. Eric and Kevin both said goodbye, and they started off back down the road. I waved to them as they left, and the sleigh rose into the air and flew out of sight. As odd as it was, the flying sleigh seemed normal to me by now. You kind of get used to this place and all its special weirdness pretty quick. I guess after you talk with a few reindeer, nothing seems strange anymore."

Chapter 21

"I knocked on the door to the little cottage," Grandma continued, "and a woman with short reddish blonde hair answered. She was only about five feet four inches tall, but her presence was commanding. She was dressed in multicolored leggings and a pink sweater and wore leather boots with small bells attached to the laces that jingled as she moved. She smiled a sweet, mischievous smile at me and said, 'You must be Miss Jane. Earl told me you would come by. Welcome; come in, and let's have a little cocoa. I hope you are hungry because I just received some fresh fudge and cookies, and they are best when you eat them while they are still warm.'

"As it turns out, I was starving. I felt like I hadn't eaten in days, even though I just had some cookies at Doc Brian's before I left. It seemed as if hours had passed, but I couldn't be sure because there were no clocks here. I still didn't know if it was day or night because the northern lights just flickered on and on. I thanked Tina and followed her inside.

"The house appeared small from the outside, but it was actually quite big. There was a fireplace in the main room, and it burned brightly, warming the air and my senses. I could smell the cocoa as it simmered on the stove, and this house had another scent that was familiar, and yet its source eluded me. It was sweet and fresh. It was subtle but still commanded my attention. I breathed it in and finally realized what it was. It was the scent of Christmas itself. It was a smell that brought back all my Christmas memories, both past and present, and wound them together till they flooded over me like a waterfall.

"I was overwhelmed with emotion and couldn't stop the tears as they found their way down my cheeks and onto my chin, where they dripped onto the fur of my parka. Tina reached out, took my hands, and sat me down on her wooden rocker, a rocker just like Earl had back in his cabin in North Pole, Alaska, where the real journey began."

* * *

For the first time since Dad and I picked the tree up at the Great Northern Christmas Spirit & Tree Co and brought it into Grandma's house, I smelled it. The smell was soft and sweet and distinct, and it mixed with the cocoa from my mug. It started filling my memories too. It brought them back in waves, waves that began to overwhelm me. I felt the warm droplets sliding down my cheeks, just like Grandma described in her story. Maybe there was more to her story than just words to fill the time. Maybe, just maybe, she knew something special and was really trying to make me understand this idea beyond the here and now. This time, I didn't interrupt her. I just let her continue, and again, I hung on every word.

* * *

"Tina asked if I was all right, and I told her that the past few days were a bit overwhelming. She seemed to understand, and that made me feel better. I instantly felt at home in her house. She was older than me, but for some reason, I felt very comfortable around her. She motioned me to the small kitchen near the back of the cabin, so I got up and followed her.

"She opened a cupboard next to her little stove and pulled out two large mugs and two plates. She put the plates on a small table sitting under the only window in the room, pulled out a tray of cookies that were warming in the oven, and set them on the table. As soon as I smelled those cookies, my stomach started to rumble. She took the cocoa off the stove and poured it straight from the pan into the mugs, without spilling a drop. She reached into a jar on the counter and added some miniature marshmallows to each one, eight to be exact. There was fudge under a glass-covered platter on the table. There were several different varieties of fudge; I couldn't wait to taste each one. Tina sat down, picked up her mug, and said, 'Here's to new friends and new adventures.' We clinked mugs, blew the steam off, and took a sip. She told me not to be shy and just dig in because we had a big day ahead of us.

"The cookies didn't have any frosting or sprinkles on them, but they were so fresh and warm, I really didn't notice. They were the best yet. After two cookies, one shaped like a Christmas tree and the other like a bell, I reached out and took a piece of the fudge. It was rich and sweet and soft, and I ate it so fast, I almost didn't taste it. Tina laughed at me as I ate, and I grew a little embarrassed, but I couldn't help myself and grabbed another piece, and we both laughed.

"We ate rather quickly, and when the mugs were empty, Tina refilled them and asked if I was ready for some exploring. I nodded yes, and she must have seen the excitement on my face because she said, 'Well, then, off we go.'

"She pulled on her pink parka and headed for the back door. I followed, and just before we went outside, I caught a whiff of the scent again, the one that brought all those memories of Christmas into my mind. I stopped her at the door and asked what that sweet smell was. She looked at me a little funny, sniffed the air, and said, 'Oh, that's just my tree. It just arrived today. I haven't decorated yet because it has to drop first.'

"I asked if she was talking about a Christmas tree, and she replied, 'Well, we just call them trees, but I guess they could be considered Christmas trees because we always get them for this time of the year. It's just a tradition we have up here. We all get one to put in our homes, and we have family and friends over to help decorate them. We use this time to get together and remember the past and prepare for the future. If you like, you can join me and my family and help us decorate mine.'

"I told her I would like that very much, and she seemed pleased and honored that I agreed. I asked where the tree was, and she said it was in the meeting room. I followed her back to the front of the house, and she opened the door to a room, and the scent of the tree filled the entire house and all my senses. I was almost overcome by its presence.

"The tree was set in a corner between the only two windows in the room, and even though it wasn't decorated, it was in full command of the room. It had a large ball at the bottom that looked like burlap. Tina said the ball was filled with the dirt the tree had grown in all of its short life. She said this was so it could be replanted in the spring. She also told me the decorations would tell the story of her family and their history.

"This really intrigued me, and I was hoping that maybe I could film this event to add to my reindeer piece, although I still doubted I could get back in time for it to air.

"We finally exited the house out the back door; Tina had a large garage and a small building next to it. The garage had two overhead doors separated by three pine pillars from the ground to the roof. There were some ski runner marks going to the side door, and it looked like it hadn't been opened in months. There was a door on the right side of the garage with footprints leading to it, as if it was the main entrance. This door faced the other building, which was just a smaller version of the stable on Nick's property. The front had a wide sliding door with a sign above it that read *Todd's Place* in the now-familiar old script and red paint. The sliding door had a rope with a knot tied on it and appeared to function like a doorknob. We walked to the garage, and Tina entered the smaller side door. She lit a lamp, which illuminated the interior of the garage. I could see the right side was filled with crafts I assumed Tina had created. She moved to the center of the garage and lit another lamp, and the rest of the garage came into view. This side had two small sleighs setting side by side. The smaller one looked like it held two people, one in front of the other. It was pink, like everything else Tina had, and it had a canvas top covering it . The second sleigh was similar to Gary's. It wasn't as big, but it was the same type. It had a bench seat in the front and a flatbed area in the back with the same low sides on it.

"Tina walked to the back of the garage; there were two doors matching the ones on the front. I went into the garage and followed Tina to the door on the left with the sleighs in it. She opened the door and outside, a reindeer was standing, like he had been waiting for the door to open all along. He looked at Tina and then to me, and Tina said, 'Oh, sorry; Todd, this is Miss Jane; Miss Jane, this is Todd.'

"Todd said, 'Good to meet you,' and walked to the front of the smaller sleigh, sliding himself into the harness. The harness was adorned with ten shiny bells that jingled as he wriggled into it. Todd asked where we were headed, and Tina said, 'Let's just start in town and see what the day brings.'

"Todd pulled the sled through the open door at the back of the garage, and I followed. Tina pulled the door shut, and we climbed aboard. Tina sat in front, and I sat in back. The seats on the sleigh were extremely comfortable, and I was happy to have the canvas canopy above us because the snow was coming down even faster than it had been. It was piling up everywhere, and I wondered how we were going to go anywhere.

"Todd pulled us through the deep snow, slowly at first. He rounded the garage and headed up the driveway. I asked Tina if everyone in this place owned a reindeer, and the sleigh stopped abruptly. Tina looked back at me through the opening in her parka, shaking her head and giving me an "Oh, no, now you've done it" look. Todd looked back at me too, but his look was a little different. He looked like he was preparing to say something to me, and it wasn't going to be very nice. I had seen that look before, and it was usually followed by a sarcastic remark aimed at putting someone in their place. I wasn't sure what was going on, but I didn't expect things to remain pleasant going forward.

"Todd didn't hesitate; he spoke right up and said, 'Yeah, Tina, does everyone in this place own reindeer?'

"I felt the sarcasm cut right through me like a cold north wind in a blizzard. Tina smiled at me, turned to Todd, and said, 'Relax, Todd. Miss Jane is new here. Give her a break and give it a rest.' He shook off the snow that was building up on him and continued to stare at me, but the look in his eyes softened somewhat, and I even thought he was beginning to smile a little.

"Todd said, 'Every time an outsider comes through, they ask the same question. I get a little sick of it. What is it with you people? Why are you always so obsessed with owning everything?'

"Tina said, 'Todd, you know things are different on the outside. Why are you always so rude to our guests? Give them a break once in a while, will ya?'

"'Hey, I am who I am,' Todd responded, and he said he was sorry. The sleigh began to move again.

"Tina explained to me that this is a community that shares all things. Everyone contributes their talents and abilities to support the entire group. The reindeer are strong and smart and provide most of the transportation needs to the town and the company."

"Todd turned and showed a wide smile, raising his head with pride. His steps became stronger, and he developed a little swagger to his gate. The bells jingled a brighter tune, and Tina winked at me like she had played this game with him before.

"Tina explained, 'The reindeer have their own accommodations; they come and go as they please and are always willing to help in any way we need. In this climate, their unique talents and abilities are vital for our survival. We help assure their comfort through the upkeep of their dwellings, and we also provide them with food and water so they remain healthy and strong. We have also forged close friendships that last a lifetime; well, with Todd, this is more of an ongoing process.' I heard her snicker, and Todd snorted a muffled laugh himself.

"With the snow growing deeper, the sleigh began to bog down. I was somewhat afraid Todd wasn't going to be able to go much farther, even though he appeared plenty strong. As we neared the end of St Tina and were about to enter the outer circle road, we picked up speed. Somehow, the sleigh seemed suddenly lighter. We continued to gain speed; Todd reared up his head, and then it happened: We were airborne. It took my breath away. I felt like I was on a roller coaster, and we had just gone over the top of the first hill. I was weightless, and before I could stop myself, I screamed, 'Weeee,' like a little girl, and it felt great. I wasn't embarrassed at all, and when we made the left turn at the outer circle road, the sleigh tilted on its side, and I could see the ground straight down over my left shoulder, once again it happened: Weeee.

"I heard Todd ask Tina if I was planning on doing this all the way, and she just gave him a dismissive wave, and we continued on. We were above the treetops, and I felt totally free for the first time in my life.

"Once again, I heard the singing before I saw him. The reindeer I now know as Stormy was making another pass through the sky. He was higher than he had been on previous sightings, and Todd commented what an odd duck he was. 'What's wrong with that guy?' he asked. 'Is he looney or something?' Tina remarked how she thought he was cute, and he had a great voice too.

"Todd told her, 'You would think that, wouldn't you?' The banter between the two of them continued until we finally landed. We flew smooth and fast, and I could see most of the town as it lay before us. The town was laid out in a large circle, with the outer circle road being its perimeter. The two bigger roads, St Nicolas and St Earl, cut the town into four equal parts. I could see there were two of the side streets, coming off the outer circle road at even distances between St Nicolas and St Earl. From our vantage point above the trees, I could see each of the side streets had small driveways leading up to log homes that dotted the interior of the town, and each section of the town was similar to this design. The pillars of smoke I had seen earlier rose from the homes and the outbuildings all throughout the land. Smoke rose gently through the falling snow, and it was beautiful. I really wish I had my camera or my video equipment. I decided I would ask Tina to take me back to the plane to retrieve it at some point in our journey.

"We passed over the roundabout and started descending, and for the first time, I saw activity all around. People waved at us as they saw us, and the other reindeer would nod at Todd as he passed. Most of the reindeer pulled sleighs of various sizes and designs. The sleighs all appeared to have been made for specialized purposes. Some had only one reindeer pulling them, while others had up to four. The area we landed in is what I would call the manufacturing district. There were shops everywhere. Each one had a distinct function and design.

"They were all made of the same pine logs as the homes, but these were more like storefronts with manufacturing buildings behind and beside them. Some of them were much bigger than the others, and each appeared to have its own theme.

"Todd stopped the sleigh directly in front of the center shop. A strong scent of chocolate filled the immediate area, and my stomach began to rumble in anticipation of a sample or two."

Chapter 22

"Tina started to climb down from the sleigh," Grandma continued, "and it jerked forward. She nearly slipped and almost fell into a tall snowbank piled on the edge of the road.

"She shouted at Todd, 'Real funny!' Todd snickered and just said, 'Sorry, my bad.'

"I don't think the *sorry* part was altogether sincere. I followed her off, and she told Todd we would see him later. He took off down the road, and up, up in the air he arose. Just like that, he was out of sight.

"There was a path cleared in the snow that led up to the porch of the storefront, and we walked up to the door. Above the door was a wooden sign that read TGNCS&T Co. Chocolates. It was painted in red and used the same old script as all the other signs I'd seen since arriving here. We stopped just outside the door. Tina noticed I was looking at the sign and asked if something was wrong. I looked at her and said, 'All the signs in this town are made of the same type wood and all are painted in red paint with the same old type script; why is that? Who created them?'

"Tina smiled a proud smile and said, "That would be me. I designed the signs. When we decided to create the company, it became our logo and the signature for our products. We use it for our labeling too. What do you think? Do you like it?"

"I said it was nice but seemed kind of outdated. When I asked if she ever thought about modernizing it, she said, 'You might be surprised at how old this company really is. We have discussed it several times, but the consensus is always the same: we want to be true to our original ideals and traditions.'

"Tina opened the door of the chocolate shop, and I heard jingle bells ring as we entered. The bells were on a leather strap hung on the inside door handle. It was just like the one my grandparents put on their door each Christmas back home. The jingling sound made me feel like I did when I visited them as a child.

"The aroma of chocolate filled the air. The entrance of the shop had a small display area with shelves behind glass. The countertop was wood and had a shiny coating on it. There were several bowls filled with different kinds of chocolates and fudge, and a sign in front of each bowl that read 'FREE SAMPLES: please try some.'

"Tina took a sample from each bowl and popped them into her mouth. I didn't want to seem greedy, so I took just one piece of fudge and ate it. I had never before tasted such sweet and rich fudge; it was almost magical. I couldn't help myself and took a piece from each bowl; without thinking twice, I popped them into my mouth. Each one was even better than the last, and after I had tried one of each, I went back to the fudge bowl and had another piece.

"An older woman came from the back of the shop and said her name was Esther. She had a kind smile and wore spectacles. Tina introduced me, and Esther came around to the front of the counter and gave me a big hug. She asked us if we would like a tour, and I accepted with great anticipation. We followed her around the counter and into the back room, which was much larger than it appeared from the outside. The smell of chocolate was so powerful, it almost made me dizzy. The first thing I noticed was how clean the room was. Everything shined like it was brand new, but I could tell it must be really, really old.

"There were enormous bowls lined up one after another on stands with wheels on them. Each bowl had a label describing what was in it. One said 'Milk Chocolate,' and another was labeled 'Dark Chocolate with Peanut Swirl.' Each one was filled three-quarters of the way up with a different delicious treat. Each bowl had a large wooden spoon, and there were several men dressed in all white from head to toe taking turns stirring the bowls. They stirred the bowls in a counter clockwise motion until all the ingredients were perfectly smooth. Once a bowl was mixed to perfection one of the men would push it into another room off to the side and they would move on to the next bowl and start mixing that one in the same counter clockwise motion. We followed Esther into the second room where they had moved the mixed bowls. This room was smaller but still surprisingly large. In this room were another man and a woman. Esther told me the man was Karl and he one of her sons and the woman's name was Donna and she was her daughter. Karl lined a bowl up to a chute and tipped it so the chocolate would run down and flow onto a large pan with several Christmas themed molds in it. Donna slid the pan with the Christmas molds in it, carefully and evenly down a conveyer and the chocolate filled each shape completely. Once it was full a second pan was pushed in place and this continued till the bowl was empty.

"The pans on the conveyer disappeared into yet another room. This room was a cooling room according to Esther but we didn't go in there. We walked past the door to this room and entered a forth door.

"When we entered the fourth room everyone looked busy. There were stacks of boxes piled everywhere and each one had TGNCS&T Co. logo printed on them in the old red script. The pans came from the cooling room and were flipped upside down onto a smooth metal table. Each figure was perfect. This room had only four people working in it and what they did, with great care and ease, was to wrap each piece of chocolate in colorful foil and pack them into different size boxes. The chocolate must have been ready for delivery at this point because they pushed the boxes down another conveyer and at the end of it was a sleigh with two reindeer hitched to it. Three men Mike, Paul and Gene, also sons of Esther's, stood at the end of the conveyer and stacked the boxes onto the sleigh. Once the sleigh was full the reindeer pulled it out a back overhead door and it disappeared. Another sleigh would then take its place with two more reindeer pulling it. It all ran smoothly.

"Esther escorted us back to the front of the shop and back to the storefront where the counter held all the samples and asked if I had any questions. As a reporter I should have had plenty but I was just so overwhelmed the only question I could think of was, could have some more samples. Tina and Esther laughed hard and when Esther finally caught her breath she said, "Take all you like." And I did. We said our goodbyes and Tina and I left.

"We walked off the porch, back to the street and on to the next store. The snow was gaining strength and Tina looked at the sky with great concern so I asked her if everything was okay. She gave me a smile and nodded yes, but once again I wasn't very reassured.

"The next store we came to was very similar in looks and size as the chocolate shop. I followed Tina up the walk and onto the porch. We went straight in and again jingle bells rang as we entered. The store also was filled with an inviting aroma but his time it was the smell of fresh baked cookies. I knew what the scent was even before we went in because above the door was another sign and this one read TGNCS&T Co Specialty Baked Goods, on it.

"Once again there was a counter, and on that counter were plates loaded with all sorts of cookies and cakes and they too had a sign that read, *FREE SAMPLES please enjoy.*

"I didn't hesitate and took a sample from each plate. I know I should have been full by now but for some reason I was able to eat them without even thinking twice. They were warm and the frosting was smooth and sweet and they were the best ones I'd had so far.

"I was enjoying the cookies when the bells on the door rang and in stepped a young woman with blonde hair. Tina turned and gave her a hug. Tina introduced her to me as Judy. Judy was the lead baker and ran the shop. She too was small but appeared strong and extremely healthy and she was very friendly. She asked if I had a chance to try any samples and I told her yes and they were by far the best cookies I have ever had. She smiled and thanked me but her smile was like the one Tina just gave me. I knew something was wrong but I was afraid to ask what it was. As it turned out I didn't have to. Tina asked Judy if Nick was back yet; Judy's smile faded, and she just shook her head.

"I knew Nick was Earl's brother and Earl was at his house right now for some sort of meeting. What I didn't know was where Nick was at or what the meeting was all about.

"Judy asked if I was up for a short tour of the bakery and I said yes.

We went out back and the bakery was set up similar to the chocolate shop. The same large metal bowls were the first things I saw. These were filled with dough and frosting instead of chocolate and fudge but still had the same wooden spoons used for stirring. There were a few women slowly mixing the bowls in same the counterclockwise motion. This counterclockwise motion seemed to be the theme of how things were done here. The big difference with this system was instead of pans with molds in them, the dough was poured onto a flat metal pan, and a rolling pin flattened the dough into a single sheet. The pan was transferred to another station, and a cutter device was pressed onto the sheet of dough. The cutter had several shapes made into it, so when it was lifted up off the dough, the tray was filled with reindeer and bells and trees and things. The pan of dough was placed into an oven, and when it was done, each cookie was frosted by hand and decorated by another group of women. The cookies were packed in plastic bags, boxed, and loaded onto waiting sleighs and pulled out by the reindeer. I could see it was all very efficient and simple.

"While we toured the bakery, I overheard Judy and Tina talking about Nick and some sort of crisis. Judy had mentioned it wasn't like Nick to be this late returning from the training. I heard Tina ask Judy about the meeting, and she said several teams were out looking for them right now, but the storm was hindering any progress.

"I asked if everything was all right, and Judy finally told me what was going on. She said Nick always went out with his team of reindeer for training. The training was to prepare them for the major deliveries they do this time every year. They need to get in shape because they have to go all night and travel far.

"I asked how long they had been gone. This was the reporter in me finally coming out. I felt my investigative side might be of some help, although I didn't know anything about this place. I didn't even know what the training they were doing involved. I guess I just wanted to be part of this place and its people in some way.

"Judy was a little reluctant to give any details, and Tina just waited for her to answer. Judy finally let me in a little. She told me they left four days ago, just as the storm was starting, and should have been home the same day. They normally go out every day for a week but return each night to rest and eat. She said they had never been gone more than a full day and night on any of the previous training runs.

"I told them everything would be okay. They were probably just holed up somewhere safe, riding the storm out. They both thanked me for saying it, but I knew they weren't so sure it was true. Judy offered us a few cookies to go, and we left.

"Back outside, the snow was still coming down. As we approached the sidewalk from the bakery, I noticed the sleighs were all being pulled on the ground. There were no reindeer or sleighs in the air at all. I know this sounds funny, but it felt strange that no one was flying anywhere. Just before we reached the street, a large sleigh loaded with small metal containers passed by. There were hundreds of them, and they were stacked ten high. The containers filled the entire cart. This sleigh had only one reindeer pulling it, which made me believe the containers were all empty. It passed us, turned down the alley that ran by the next store, and disappeared behind the big building out back. Tina said those were the containers they filled with the cocoa. They were made one at a time by a craftsman named Norman. He worked every day just to keep up with the supply, because the cocoa was always in such high demand. His wife Carrie and the rest of his family made the actual cocoa itself, and it was a very secretive process.

"The cocoa was my favorite thing of all, and just thinking about it made my mouth water. We stopped into the store, and the bells jingled on the door. The counter was like a big stove with three pots on top. The pots had steam softly rising from them; the sweet aroma of cocoa filled the air.

"A young woman, Carrie herself, was carefully stirring them one at a time in a smooth counterclockwise direction. She looked up at us and smiled. She asked Tina if there was any word yet, and Tina shook her head no. The woman stopped stirring, took a pan from the counter, and asked if we were thirsty. I nodded a hearty yes, and she pulled three mugs from behind the counter and began to fill them, one at a time. She reached into a jar, plopped eight miniature marshmallows into each one of them, and slid a mug to Tina and one to me. She took the third mug and raised it and said, 'Here's to a quick and safe return of Nick and the team.'

"We raised ours mugs in return and blew the steam off the top and took a drink. This was the sweetest and richest cocoa yet.

"Tina introduced me to her, and we all took another drink. She looked kind, but I could tell she was somewhat stressed too. She apologized to me in advance and said that she would not be able to give us a tour of her shop because the storm had slowed production, and everything was backing up. She said that after the Celebration of the Light was over, she would be happy to give us the grand tour. We finished our cocoa, thanked her, and left.

"We went back outside into the growing snowstorm, and I heard him again. Stormy was somewhere in the sky, singing those familiar Christmas songs. I looked up and couldn't see anything but the falling snow. Tina said Stormy must be crazy or something because no one in their right mind would be flying in this weather. I could hear jingle bells coming down the street, and after a minute, Todd pulled up in Tina's pink canvas-covered sleigh. He stopped directly in front of the cocoa store and told us we had to get in.

"Tina asked him what was up, and he said he would explain on the way but we had to go right now.

"We climbed aboard the sleigh, and Todd trotted off. He didn't take flight because of the storm, but he was pulling as fast as he could. I was somewhat disappointed because I wanted to feel the freedom of flying in the sleigh once again.

Chapter 23

Grandma said, "Tina didn't wait long before she asked what the problem was."

"Todd kept pulling and without breaking stride, he said, 'We're needed at Nick's place. Earl sent out a request for an emergency meeting. Every one of the elders is going to be there. That's all I know.'

"We continued down the outer road till we came to St. Nicolas, and without slowing down, Todd pulled a hard left. We entered the roundabout and crossed St Earl and kept going on St Nicolas. I was sure we were going to crash in the roundabout or maybe flip over or something, but we made it through somehow.

"We arrived at Nick's home, and there were sleighs everywhere. We stopped at the walk, and the other reindeer started asking Todd what was going on. He shook his head, and it looked like he even shrugged his shoulders, as if to say he didn't know.

"I followed Tina up the walk and onto the porch, and without even knocking, we opened the door and entered the house. It was filled with people. They were all talking excitedly. The house smelled of cookies and fudge and cocoa and, of course, pine tree.

"Standing in the center of the main room was a huge pine tree. This tree looked to be permanent. It didn't have a brown bag around the trunk. It looked as if it grew right out of the floor. As I looked at it, I imagined the tree was here first, and the house was built around it.

"I looked around and saw the house was full. This was a large house compared to the ones I had seen around town; the living room was huge, even with the pine tree growing up out of the floor. There were at least fifteen people in it, talking to each other. Earl was at the center of the group; he appeared to be in charge. Gary was on his left, and next to Gary stood Judy. Tina went and stood to Earl's right. I saw Carrie standing next to a young man I figured was Norman, the tin container maker. Other people were standing around, some of whom I had seen on sleighs or working in the stores I had visited. Even Doc Brian and Kelly were there. Doc Brian strolled over to me and asked how I was feeling. He took a look at my wound under my bandage and said, 'Well, it looks like you will live.'

"Earl called for order, and the group began to quiet down. Doc Brian returned to Kelly, and I stayed back out of the way and just listened. Earl thanked everyone for being there, especially during these busy times. He went on to say he knew everyone was concerned about Nick. He said even though Nick and his team had never been gone for this long and the storm was really bad, they should not lose hope that he and the team would be all right. He reassured the group that everything would continue to proceed as usual, and as soon as there was the slightest break in the weather, the search teams would be back in the air until they were found.

"No one seemed comforted by his speech. He went on to say the best thing everyone could do right now was to continue with their normal routines, including the traditional tree decorating tonight at the beginning of the Celebration of the Light which kicked off the Christmas celebrations. Earl added if they waited for Nick, it could throw off the timing of the Big Trip, and if that happened, everyone would be affected, not just them.

"The young man I assumed was Norman added, 'That is, if there even is a Big Trip at all.' By the looks on the faces of those gathered here, it was obvious he wasn't the only one thinking it.

"Right then, a feeling of sadness and fear came over me. I'm not sure why I felt this way because I didn't know Nick or what the Big Trip was, but at that moment, I felt I was a part of it all.

"Earl started to talk business. He was asking about production levels and quality and other things in order to refocus the group and take their minds off Nick and the team, so I decided to slip out and explore the grounds, starting with the big barn.

"Outside, the conversation was similar to what was going on in the house. The reindeer had unhitched themselves from their sleighs and gathered in front of the barn. Todd was near the front, and Eric and Kevin were by his side. There were three groups in front of them, and they were reporting on search grids and making plans to continue the search as soon as the weather allowed.

"One of the groups of reindeer brought up the subject of Stormy. Eric said he hadn't seen or heard Stormy since earlier in the day. Kevin added that when the search continued, they should try to find Stormy and get him back on the ground so we didn't have two crises going on, and everyone agreed.

"I slipped past and walked around to the side of the barn with the stalls. I counted eight separate accommodations in all. I continued around the back and saw a large door that opened upwards. There were some old ski tracks coming from under the door and disappearing into the deeper snow. I noticed a smaller door on the other side of the large door and decided to take a look inside. I opened the door, but it was dark inside. It was a small room, like an office of some sort. There was a fire burning in a small pot belly stove; it gave off heat for the room but provided no illumination.

"I entered cautiously, as my eyes adjusted to the lack of light. I could make out the form of a single desk and chair on one wall near the stove. Boxes were stacked around the desk and against the adjacent wall. I could see a faint glow on the desk, so I carefully made my way over to it and found it was an oil lamp. I found the wick adjuster and turned it up. The flame grew larger and brighter, and the room filled with a soft light. I had to blink a couple of times so that my eyes could adjust to the sudden increase in light.

"The room wasn't real big, maybe fifteen feet deep and twenty-five feet wide, with a low ceiling only seven or eight feet high. The room was warm due to the heat radiating off the little stove. Next to the stove was a neatly piled stack of wood, split into small pieces just the right size to fit into the stove. There was a faint pine sent mixed with the smell of smoke from the wood stove.

"On the desk lay several papers like invoices or receipts. They were in two separate piles.

"The receipts had names and locations on them but nothing else. Nothing distinguished one from another except the piles they were in. As my eyes adjusted to the light some more, I recognized the boxes stacked against the wall. These boxes matched the ones I had seen on the plane as we traveled through the storm and into the northern lights, just after I had hit my head. Those green and red boxes were very similar to the ones right in front of me by this desk, the ones Earl seemed concerned with me seeing as I left the plane and the one red box in particular, which had popped open and had a receipt with my name on it. What is the purpose of these boxes? Why were there green ones and red ones? What did this have to do with the Great Northern Christmas Spirit & Tree Co., and how did they get my name?

"I was startled by a voice in the doorway saying, 'Hey, you shouldn't be in here. You need to get out like now.' It was Kevin, and behind him was his brother Eric. They both shook their heads at me and Eric added, 'This is Nick's private office; the only people who go in here are Nick and Earl.'

"I was scared and a little embarrassed because I was in there without permission, so I turned the lamp wick back down and left the room, closing the door behind me. I told Kevin and Eric I was sorry, and they suggested I not tell anyone I had been in there or what I saw. I agreed, and we made our way back to the main house."

Chapter 24

"As we came around to the front of the barn," Grandma continued, "I saw the reindeer pulling themselves back into their harnesses and aligning their sleighs so they could leave quickly fashion.

"The meeting must have come to an end because the people who had gathered were leaving the house. Earl shook hands with each person as they left and gave them some kind of reassuring comment. Doc Brian and Kelly left first, followed by Norman and Carrie. One by one, they all climbed into their respective sleighs and headed on their way. The only ones left at the end were Tina, Gary, and Earl.

"Tina came up to me and said that she and Todd were going to get prepared for the tree trimming; I could go with Earl and meet up with her later. I agreed, and she gave me a hug and climbed into her sleigh. Todd gave me a nod, and they left me standing near the porch. As Eric and Kevin began climbing into their harnesses, Earl called me to come back into the house. He looked tired and sad, and I'm not sure why, but I gave him a hug and told him everything was going to be all right.

"As I let go of him, I saw the smile return to his face, and I believed what I had said. Gary went around dimming the lamps, and after adding a few logs to the fireplaces, he met up with us at the tree in the living room.

"We stood there in an eerie silence, and the tree started to glow. It grew brighter by the second. It was as if someone had just plugged in a strand of lights, and they twinkled brightly in the branches. I was mesmerized by the beauty. Earl turned to me and said, 'The Celebration of the Light has begun; the winter solstice is upon us.'

"I must have had a confused look on my face because Earl said to me, 'This is when the sun reaches its farthest point from the North Pole. It creates an electromagnetic charge here, intensifying the effect of the aurora borealis. For the next ten days, the northern lights will glow brighter than at any other time of the year; it is our tradition to decorate our trees on this day and gather with family and friends to celebrate the Christmas holiday and the spirit of love for one another this holiday brings to the people all around the earth. Partway through the celebration, my brother Nick loads his sleigh with gifts, and he and his team deliver them to deserving people throughout the globe. He created this tradition after we settled here and found out that the reindeer here could fly.'

"We headed outside, and Gary stayed behind. Eric and Kevin were all hitched up and ready to go. It was nearly as light as midday now, and I could see the northern lights burning brightly all around us. I think we all noticed it at the same time, but Earl was the first to say it, 'The storm is letting up. We need to get the search parties back in the air. Let's spread the word; have everyone gather at the plane.'

"Eric and Kevin took off without hesitation, and we were airborne. The thrill came back instantly, and 'Weeee' was all that came out of my mouth. The three of them burst out in laughter, and we glided effortlessly across the sky. I could see the smoke pillars again as we passed over the cabins and homes along the way.

"Eric called for the search teams to assemble and meet at the plane. The response was instantaneous. I saw reindeer taking off and heading to the area where we had landed and stored the plane, and we made one last pass over the town.

"We landed outside the barn where the plane was stored, and Earl gathered the search teams together. They made a plan and dispersed in all directions. Earl climbed back on the sleigh, and just before we took off, I asked if I could retrieve my camera equipment from the plane. He thought about it for a minute and then climbed down and went in the barn. He returned with my camera bag and handed it up to me. I looked inside and saw everything in it except the still camera. That's when I remembered I had my still camera around my neck before I was taken to Doc Brian's; I would have to retrieve it later. I pulled the video camera out and loaded a fresh tape into the slot, checked the battery, and told Earl I was ready. He told Eric and Kevin to head to Tina's. I pushed the Record button, and we were off once again; up, up, and away we went.

"The scenery through the eyepiece was incredible. The northern lights made the snow sparkle and shine in the trees like a trillion twinkling Christmas lights burning all at once. I filmed Eric and Kevin guiding the sleigh through the air with the greatest of skill and ease. When we landed at Tina's, Earl and I got off the sleigh, and Tina met us at the door. Her family and some of her friends were already there. She invited us in. The smell of pine needles mixed with sweet cocoa and fresh cookies brought the joy back to my heart and filled me with hope, but it also made me feel a little homesick too. Once again, I longed to be home with my own family and sharing Christmas like we used to when I was still a young girl.

"Inside Tina's cabin, the fireplace was burning brightly and warm. We took our coats and gloves off, and Tina led us to the viewing room, where the tree stood proudly. All around were boxes of bulbs and assorted decorations. Each box had the logo of the Great Northern Christmas Spirit & Tree Co. written on it in the familiar old script and red ink.

"A young man brought us some cocoa and cookies. I took two cookies shaped like bells. They were warm and soft; I was starving, so they didn't last long. The cocoa was steaming and smelled so sweet, I couldn't wait for a taste. I blew the steam off the top, saw the eight miniature marshmallows floating on the top, and took a long sip. The group of people who were gathered sat in a semicircle around the tree, cocoa in hand and waiting.

"Tina opened the first box and pulled out four ornaments. Two were silver, and two were gold. Each pair had a round ball and a pear-shaped one. She took the round bulbs and placed one on each side of the tree on the bottom branches and added the pear-shaped ones to the outside of the round ones on the same branches so the tree had silver bulbs on the left and golden bulbs on the right. She then closed the box and set it aside. Next, she opened another box of bulbs, and the young man who had brought us the cocoa pulled six pink bulbs out of the box. These bulbs were all round and were of three different sizes. He took his time and placed the bulbs up and down different branches from the center of the tree, taking great care that they did not set outside of the silver and gold ones. When he was finished putting his bulbs on the tree, he closed the box and set it with the other one. The next box went to young Racheal. Racheal's mother was Beth, and Beth was Tina's cousin. I watched as Racheal removed a bulb from her box. There were about twelve bulbs total in the box; they were pink with silver stripes running through them. Each one of them was of a different size and shape. Racheal placed the bulb she had picked just above the two silver ones from before. She pulled another bulb out and handed it to a real young boy, who was sitting eagerly up front by the tree. This boy placed his bulb as high as he could reach, on the same side of the tree as the silver ones, and pulled another bulb out of the box and handed it to a young girl, and she hung hers. This went on until all the bulbs from the box had been placed on the silver side of the tree. The next box of bulbs was pink with gold stripes, and they were placed by various family members and friends on the golden bulb side of the tree.

"After all the bulbs were hung in their respected places and the boxes closed and stored, the boxes with the specialty ornaments were opened. These boxes contained assortments of jingle bells like the ones I had seen on the doors of the shops and attached to the reindeer collars. They were in various sizes, and some were much older than the others. The size and age gave each one of them distinct tones when they jingled. This part of the tree trimming was a free-for-all. Everyone grabbed two or three bells and had the freedom to place them anywhere on the tree that they chose. The noise level in the room steadily rose as laughter and conversation grew with each bell that was hung. When the box of bells was empty and put away, another specialty box was opened. This one contained handmade ornaments. Wooden ones were carved in the shapes of presents and tied with pink bows, and some had pictures of children shellacked on them with dates engraved onto them. Last but certainly not least were the ones in the shapes of reindeer. Each reindeer had a leather collar hanging around its neck with a name written on it in old script and red ink. Tina handed these to the youngest of the group, and they took great pride in hanging the reindeer ornaments where they could be seen from any angle.

"After the wooden ornaments had been hung, Beth and Racheal looked over at Racheal's dad Rob and smiled. Rob took the hint and picked up a box wrapped in fancy colorful paper with a ribbon tied around it and a label that read 'GNCS&T Co Hard Candies.' He handed the box to Tina, and she smiled and gave all three of them a hug. She untied the ribbon and carefully removed the fancy paper and laid it aside with the label. She opened the box; inside were red and white candy canes. Perfect candy canes. She went around the room and handed each of the young children two candy canes. The kids took one and hung it on the tree and kept the other for themselves. As they were hanging the canes on the tree, Tina passed the others to everyone else.

"The last thing to be put on the tree was tinsel. My mother always said when tinsel was put on the tree, it came alive. Tinsel gave the tree character, she would say; it somehow told a story. Tina announced there were more cookies and cocoa in the other room, and everyone took it as a hint and left the viewing room. Earl was the last one out, and he closed the door behind him, leaving Tina alone with the tree and the tinsel.

"We talked and laughed and drank cocoa from our mugs. I ate more cookies and even enjoyed some fudge. The doors to the viewing room finally opened, and we were given our first peek at the completed tree. It was finally finished, but with the tinsel on it, it looked dark, almost somber. I was disappointed, and I think Earl could see it on my face. He came over and whispered in my ear, 'Just wait for it.'

"I wasn't sure what he meant, when suddenly Tina pulled the curtains open from the windows on each side of the tree, and the northern lights invaded the dimness of the room. The strands of tinsel lit up as if they were on fire. Each strand shimmered in red, blue, green, and white. The tree began to glow, and as if someone had given a signal, the whole house erupted in song. Christmas carols echoed throughout the room and filled the halls, and I felt like it was my first Christmas ever. I couldn't stop myself from joining in the singing, and I could almost bet this was the first time I had sung a Christmas carol since I was in choir back in school.

"After a few songs, Tina approached me and asked what I thought of the tree.

"I told her it was beautiful, almost overwhelming. I asked how they decided what decorations went where and why. Her reply changed the way I thought about tree decorating, and I use this same technique to this day."

* * *

As I continued listening to Grandma's story, I thought about her tree. I looked at it and saw it was almost the same as the one she had described at Tina's house. It stood by the window. We choose the bulbs by color, size, and shape. We place them according to a grand design, and then we add the specialty ornaments and finally the tinsel. All of this takes place before we plug it in and turn on the lights. When the lights are turned on, the tree finally comes to life. The only thing she hadn't explained in this story was Stormy, even though I thought the whole reason she was telling it was to explain why we have this reindeer as our tree topper. I would wait and see if maybe Tina had the answer.

* * *

"Tina asked if I had seen the trees in her yard," Grandma continued, "and everyone else's yards throughout the town. I told her yes, and she asked what I noticed about the trees. I thought about it for a minute and answered, 'The colors. The colors on each street were all the same but were different from street to street. You have pink, but on St Earl, the bulbs were blue, and Doc Brian's neighborhood has mostly purple ones. The ones at Nick's house and at the roundabout were a mixture of all the colors.'

"Tina said that was right; she asked why I thought it was that way. I just shrugged my shoulders.

"She explained that each family has its own color to remind them of where they came from. This helps remind them of their past and helps them focus on the traditions from their homelands and their families."

* * *

There's that word again: tradition. It keeps coming up over and over. I guess when Dad or Grandma gives me an answer with "because it's tradition" as part of it, maybe, just maybe, it is the real answer. Maybe the adult thing to do would be to ask what the tradition is and how and where it started. Huh; this may be my first real adult thought.

* * *

Grandma continued, "Tina said the way we decorate our trees represents our families. The gold and silver bulbs at the bottom represent our grandparents and parents, the gold ones for the man's side of the family, and the silver for the woman's. The striped ones are the rest of the family: brothers and sisters, aunts and uncles, cousins and second cousins, and such. The specialty ornaments are the mementos of our lives, and the bells are for our friends. The tinsel was added some time later when we started to bring the trees into our homes to decorate. This helped to recreate the beauty of the icicles that accumulated on the trees outside and reflected the northern lights in a dazzling display.

"Grandma said the only other thing in common about all the trees was there are no tree toppers on any of them. Back at my parents, we had an angel topper on our tree, and some of our neighbors had stars or even ribbons in the shape of bows on them. I asked Tina if they used tree toppers here?"

"She said they certainly did. They add a new one every year to give special recognition to someone who has done something extraordinary for the community. Nick and Earl took nominations every year. They made recommendations to the elders, and the elders brought the recommendations to their respective communities, and a vote is taken. After a candidate is confirmed, Earl contacts her, and she creates an image representing the winner. This was her gift to the community. Just as Robert, Beth, and Racheal give out the candy canes, or Carrie the sweet cocoa, or even Doc Brian and Kelly taking care of those who were injured or ill, this was her gift to thank everyone for being in her life.

"I asked Tina what Earl and Nick gave.

"She said, 'Earl is a woodsman. He grows the trees and supplies us with logs for our homes and wood for our fires to heat and cook with. Earl was actually our first tree topper because he found a way for us to bring the trees into our homes for decorating without having to cut them down. His burlap root bag idea sustained them until they could be replanted and have a full life. While you were recovering at Doc Brian's, he and Gary, along with the help of some of the reindeer, delivered these trees to everyone and set them up so we could decorate tonight.'

"Tina explained that Nick was the one who brought them together with the reindeer. He found a way to help and protect them, and in return, they became one of the most important parts of the community. The friendship he formed with them helped to stabilize this town. He and his team of reindeer, eight in all, are revered for their giving hearts; every year during the celebration, they load up his special sleigh and deliver the things produced here across the whole of the earth."

Chapter 25

Grandma said, "As Tina was explaining these things to me, there was a large commotion outside. We looked out the window and saw the first of the search teams returning. They were headed for the roundabout, and as they circled, people were migrating that way.

"Earl said we needed to get down there and find out what was happening. Everyone began putting on their coats and mittens, and outside, the reindeer climbed into their harnesses. Tina and I boarded her pink canvas-covered sleigh, and Todd was ready to go instantly. We took off first, and Eric and Kevin had Earl in tow right behind us.

"Sleighs began landing everywhere, and the groups started gathering around the main tree. The first search party waited till Earl was in place, and then they reported directly to him. The older one spoke first. His name was Shawn. He and his younger brother Thomas talked to Earl for a few minutes, and the second search team arrived. These were Shawn and Thomas's brothers. Their names were Corey and Jayme. They too spoke with Earl. The only one of the search party who wasn't back yet was Joshua. Joshua was the middle brother of the five and tended to go off on his own.

"Earl searched the skies for his return, along with everyone else. After a few minutes, the crowd started to mumble amongst themselves, and Earl raised his hands and asked for calm and quiet. A hush came over the group, and the silence created an atmosphere of anticipation. I could hear my heart pounding and felt it sinking at the same time.

"There was another sound. This sound broke the silence that

enveloped the community. It was barely audible at first. Everyone craned their necks and strained to find out where the sound came from. The sound grew stronger by the seconds, but the seconds felt like an eternity. I wasn't the first to distinguish what it was, but when I finally did, I started to cry and laugh at the same time. It was a song, but not just any song. It was a Christmas carol. It was soft at first but steadily gained power. I still couldn't tell where it was coming from, but I definitely knew *who* it was coming from.

"Kevin was the first to say it but everyone else was thinking it. 'Stormy,' he blurted out. 'It's Stormy.'

"The beautiful song grew louder and louder, and I began to hear another sound. It was the sound of bells. And not just any bells; they were jingle bells, and lots of them too. The bells mixed with Stormy's singing and filled the sky with music.

"Earl was the first to spot the group. He pointed into the sky above the crowd. Everyone turned to see, and there they were. The first to come into view was the team, strong and proud and eight in all. The reindeer were pulling a huge red sleigh. Sitting high atop the sleigh in a seat made just for him was a lone rider. He held the reins loosely and guided the team with gentle compassion. He was dressed all in red, from head to toe, and wore black boots. A black belt hung around his rather large waist. It was Nick himself.

"Alongside the sleigh flew another reindeer. He just flew along, keeping pace with the others. It was Joshua, the final member of the search party. Following the sleigh were three more reindeer. The two in the front were older than the third. The third one was singing loudly and clearly. That one was Stormy, the singing reindeer who has been crossing the skies ever since I arrived.

"As the team began to circle toward the gathered crowd, I began to hear another sound. This sound was very distinctive, soft and muffled at first, but it erupted into a roar and rose to blend with the sounds of the bells and the song. This was the sound of cheering; I was part of this sound, and it felt great.

"The entire group was filled with tears of joy and laughter. I glanced up at Earl and saw the look of relief returning to his eyes. His smile caused a twinkle to appear in his eyes, which were soon filled with tears, the same tears of joy everyone else was experiencing. He gave me a quick wink as he made his way into the crowd.

"The crowd began to move left and right, creating an opening in front of the tree adorning the center of the roundabout. This gave way to a makeshift landing strip.

"The team of eight reindeer made one last circle above us and then set down in the small clearing. Joshua flew over and past the landing party and joined his brothers at the edge of the crowd. The other three reindeer circled one more time, looking for a safe place to land. It was obvious they didn't have the same landing skills as the team of eight.

"The reindeer surrounding the circle of joyous townsfolk began to gather at the outer edge of the roundabout and created a landing area of their own. They began shouting encouragement to Stormy and the other two reindeer, and the three came in for a landing, with Stormy leading the way. It wasn't pretty and looked a little dangerous, but they did finally get to the ground, and another huge cheer went up.

"As quickly as the noise had erupted, it died down just as fast, and it was silent again. All the attention quickly turned to the young singing reindeer. There was a panicked call for Doc Brian, and then another and another. At first, I couldn't tell what the crisis was, but as Doc Brian responded with Kelly at his side, a gap opened in the reindeer that encircled the three strangers. I could now see the cause of the commotion. One of the new reindeer had collapsed. It was Stormy. He was down, and I couldn't detect any movement from him at all. I remember wondering why he wasn't singing.

"Earl and the larger gentleman with the red suit and black boots, Nick, also joined Doc Brian and Kelly. Everyone looked on in horror and fear for the young buck. Earl called to Eric and Kevin to bring their sleigh; they must have anticipated this because they were already harnessed up and moving in that direction. The two other reindeer that had arrived with Stormy looked on in fear, as Kelly and Doc Brian loaded Stormy's motionless body onto the sleigh. Earl and Nick climbed in front. With all aboard, Eric and Kevin wasted no time and took flight; the sleigh flew fast and smooth toward Doc Brian's place.

"The five brothers from the search party approached the remaining two reindeer, and after Shawn spoke to them, they all took off in pursuit of the sleigh that held Stormy. They surrounded them and guided them as if they were guarding precious cargo, and they too disappeared.

"The joy and elation, so strong just a few moments before, was now all gone. The scene was now one of worry, and the mood had grown quite somber. The group was talking amongst themselves, and all thoughts had turned to Stormy. We didn't know what had happened to Nick and the team, but no one was concerned with those things for the time being. Gary took the lead this time. He talked with Tina and made an announcement.

"Gary told everyone that Doc Brian had things well in hand. We had to trust his skills and compassion. Gary said he was going to take the team back to Nick's and make sure they were cared for so they'd be ready for the Big Journey. He suggested we all go back to our responsibilities and make sure we were ready when the time came. He thanked us all for our support and concern and assured us he would pass on any information on Stormys condition as soon as it was available."There was a lot of nodding, and as everyone prepared to disperse and return to their respective duties, I could see them consoling and encouraging each other. I was thinking to myself, *If more people were like this, the world would be a much better place, indeed.*"

Chapter 26

"Everyone had gone their own way," Grandma continued. "The only ones left were Gary, Tina, Todd, the team, and me. Tina said she had a lot to do, but I was welcome to tag along, or Todd could take me around town. Gary said if I wanted to, I could ride with him and help with the team. I decided to go with him. I wanted to ride in this sleigh. I wanted to be pulled by *the* team.

"I thanked Todd, and he and Tina were on their way. Gary gestured for me to climb aboard, and I scurried onto the sleigh. Just sitting there with those eight reindeer hitched up in front of me, I knew that this was no ordinary sleigh and these were no ordinary reindeer, even for this place. Gary climbed up next to me and told me to hold on. I braced myself and Gary shouted, 'Home, gentleman,' and in an instant, we were airborne, and in another instant, we were landing at Nick's. There was no time to think and no time to blink. I didn't even get the chance to let out even a little 'Weeee.'

"There were already two reindeer in front of the barn, waiting for us. As soon as we landed, the team guided the sleigh to the large front door of the barn. Gary jumped to the ground and started to help them get out of their harnesses.

"The two reindeer who were here when we arrived moved to the side of the barn where the eight reindeer stalls were. They began pulling the ropes that functioned as doorknobs with their teeth, opening them one by one.

"I climbed down from the sleigh, approached Gary, and asked him how I could help. He told me the first thing we needed to do was brush the snow and ice off the reindeer so they could get inside and warm up. He said there were brushes in the main barn hanging on the wall to the right. I pulled open the big door on the front of the barn, revealing a huge room the size of a small warehouse. Inside were three doors on the left wall, which must have led to the other side of the barn, and one near the back.

"I found the brushes hanging on the wall and brought two of them out to the waiting reindeer. Gary had them all unhitched; the harnesses with their bells were stretched out in the back of the sleigh.

"I handed Gary one of the brushes and kept the other. I watched as Gary took the brush and began brushing one of the reindeer. He started at the top and gently stroked the fur, pulling the snow and ice off as he went along. The reindeer moaned softly with each stroke, and Gary proceeded across the back and down each leg until all the snow and ice were removed. I started on the next reindeer and tried to be as gentle as I could. 'Thank you,' the reindeer moaned as I pulled the brush across his fur. As I was brushing the snow off the front part of his neck, it revealed a leather collar with a name carved into it in the same script and colored with red ink. The name was Blitzen, and I froze.

"The reindeer asked me what was wrong, and I just stood there and looked at him with disbelief. The reindeer named Blitzen asked if I was all right.

"I nodded yes, even though I don't think I really was. I think I was somewhat in shock. I had been thinking about it all along, but now, I was faced with the reality of where I was and who I was with. It became all too real: flying reindeer, red sleigh, and a man in a red suit preparing for a worldwide trip. It was almost overwhelming. All the dreams, all the stories, all the magic, and now I had to come to grips with its reality.

"Gary started on another reindeer, and I continued with Blitzen. I finally introduced myself, and he continued to thank me and moan softly until all the snow was off of him.

"The two reindeer who were here before we had arrived came over and took up positions on each side of Blitzen. They helped him as he made his way to his stall. I could tell by the way Blitzen was walking he was completely exhausted. The other two reindeer were almost carrying him. The one to his right said, 'Steady, my friend; we got you,' and then he said to the one on the left, 'Keep him steady, Jerome.'" Jerome replied, 'I got my side, Marty; make sure you got yours.'

"This back-and-forth banter went on with each reindeer they guided to the barn and must have been normal between the two of them; nobody besides me seemed to notice it.

"As Jerome and Marty guided the last of the team to their respective accommodations, Gary handed me his brush and followed Marty and Jerome to the side of the barn. I cleaned the brushes and hung them back up in the barn and followed Gary, who was giving each one of the team an apple to eat and was making sure they all had fresh food and water. As he finished each one, Marty would use the knotted rope handle to pull the door closed. They did all this as if it were a practiced and preset routine. This obviously was not the first time this team had come home completely exhausted and had to be helped in. I figured this must be how it was every year after they made that journey I heard about. Almost immediately, I could hear the sounds of deep sleep from the reindeer (they snore really loud, just so you know).

"When the last of the doors were shut and all were snoring contently, Gary motioned me to follow him back to the sleigh. As I walked along the side of the barn, I looked up and read the signs above each door; not surprisingly, each one was familiar. All eight names were familiar, as if they were old friends, but up until today, they were just legends, myths, stories told for entertainment.

"Jerome and Marty were already at the front of the sleigh. They slipped into two small harnesses attached to the front of the sleigh. These harnesses had no bells adorning them and weren't set up for airborne travel. They were designed more for moving a sleigh short distances.

"Gary took two brooms off the wall of the barn and gave one to me. He started brushing the sleigh down, knocking the snow and ice off it. He started at the front and worked his way down the right side. I took the hint and started brushing the left side and worked my way to the back. After Gary finished his side, he climbed up and started the top and inside area of the sleigh. When I finished the left side, I started on the back, knocking the snow off of it from the top down. That's when I saw the wooden letters attached to the back of the sleigh with brass rivets. The letters were eight to ten inches high and about six inches wide. They were carved in the same old script I had seen on all the Great Northern Christmas Spirit & Tree Co. logos. The only real difference with these letters was the color. These letters were white and not the familiar red used everywhere else in town.

"The first letter I uncovered was a capitol S. As I continued to clean next to it, I discovered the second letter: a capital A. I felt heat building up on my body, and it wasn't because it was warming up outside or I was working all that hard. It was because of the anticipation building inside of my mind. I started to brush faster, and within seconds, three more white letters were revealed. The next was a capital N, followed by a capital T and a capital A. I read it a few times in my mind. 'SANTA' is what it said. Straightforward; it said 'S A N T A.' I muttered it to myself a few times, but I must have been talking louder than I thought because Gary stopped cleaning and looked at me. Marty and Jerome turned and looked at me too.

"I finally blurted, 'This is Santa's sleigh.' There was dead silence, and my words echoed into the trees and beyond.

"The silence returned, and then the laughter began. It started as a snicker from Jerome and a snort from Marty, and by the time Gary joined in, the laughter had become loud and uncontrolled, and it made me feel even hotter. I was stunned and embarrassed by the laughter and didn't know what to say or do. When it finally died down, Gary told me to keep cleaning. I didn't know what else to do, so I started brushing again, and more letters appeared. These letters were much smaller and ran down the back of the sleigh below the larger ones. 'South Arctic Natural Timber Association' is what it read, after all the snow was cleaned off. I felt like a fool for proclaiming this to be Santa's sleigh, and it was never mentioned by Gary or the two reindeer again.

"I finished the back of the sleigh, and Gary climbed down and handed me his broom. I took them and put them back in the barn. As I emerged from the barn, Gary was looking the sleigh over for any damage that may have occurred. He deemed it fit for use and asked Jerome and Marty to put it away.

"Jerome looked at me and said, 'I could pull this sleigh all by myself if I had to.' Marty shot him a look and mumbled under his breath, 'Yeah, right.'

"They maneuvered the big red sleigh with ease and skill, and within minutes, it was stored in the barn. Gary removed the short harnesses Jerome and Marty had used to put the sleigh away and hung them next to the brushes and brooms. He took the main harness from the back of the sleigh and put it in the room behind the first door behind the sleigh. I peered into this room as he opened the door. Even though it was dimly lit inside, I could see some sort of a workbench with spare bells and straps on it. I also saw a stack of cloths and some jars of a paste. My best guess was this was some sort of repair room or tack room, as I had heard them called.

"Gary returned from the room and shut the door behind him. We left the barn, and Gary closed the big door. Jerome and Marty disappeared around the far side of the barn, and I heard the faint sound of jingle bells. They emerged pulling a small four-seater sleigh and stopped right next to us. Gary motioned for me to climb aboard, and he followed. We were off the ground almost as quick as we started moving, and this time, I was able squeal out a little 'Weeee.'"

Chapter 27

Grandma said, "I could tell Jerome was proud to make me squeal because he took a quick glimpse back at me and had a big smile on his face. Marty, however, was all business. We climbed high enough to see most of the town, circling counterclockwise till we were lined up with Doc Brian's place. It was a fast trip, and we landed smoothly right out front. Eric and Kevin were there, and so was Todd. He was still hooked up to Tina's little pink sleigh. We climbed down from our sleigh, and Gary asked Eric if he had heard anything yet. Eric shook his head no, so we proceeded to the door.

"Tina opened the door before we even reached the porch. I couldn't tell how things were going by her facial expression, so we just followed her inside. Everything looked the same as when I had left there earlier in the week. We followed Tina down the hall and past the bathroom. We passed the room I stayed in while recovering from my injuries and went to a door in the back. Tina opened the door, which led us back outside, where there was another barn. This one had three of the sliding doors similar to the ones on Nick's barn. There was light coming from all three doors. We passed by them and entered a regular door near the end of the barn. The room inside was well lit, and Kelly was sitting at a desk, writing on a pad of paper. She looked up and waved us in. Tina and Gary asked if we could go back, and Kelly smiled and nodded yes. The fact that she smiled brought some comfort to me.

"We entered a large area that was neat and clean but appeared more barn than house. It was like a waiting room in a veterinarian's office. It had some wooden benches and chairs sprinkled about and an area set aside for animals. The animal section had a wooden floor full of nicks and scrapes, probably made by the hooves of reindeer milling back and forth while waiting to see Doc Brian.

"There were two reindeer in the room when we arrived; they were the ones who returned with Nick and the team. They were the same two reindeer who had left the roundabout with the search team after Doc Brian and Nick took Stormy away. These two reindeer looked worried and concerned.

"Gary approached them and introduced himself Tina and me. They looked us over, and the female said, 'Hi, I'm Audrey. This is my husband, Steve. We are Theodore's parents.' Steve gave us a small nod. I asked, 'Who is Theodore?' Steve replied that Theodore was the young reindeer who had collapsed earlier.

"'So Theodore is Stormy,' I said to Gary, and he nodded. In a kind and soothing voice, Tina asked if there was any news on Theodore, and both Steve and Audrey lowered their heads slowly and shook them no.

"I didn't mean to sound crass, but the reporter in me finally came through, and I asked what happened and how they got here.

"Audrey turned and was about to answer when Steve started to tell the story: 'As winter starts to take hold,' he began, 'we trek hundreds of miles seeking shelter from the brutal cold and relentless snows. We search for food to sustain us during the long winter months. We were about halfway to a place that has supplied us with these necessities in the past when we began to hear this low droning noise above us.'

"The plane, I thought. The noise they were hearing was Earl's plane flying over so I could get the video for my TV special.

"He continued, 'The noise suddenly changed. It grew louder and was coming closer. A panic ensued, and reindeer were darting everywhere. In the mayhem, we heard some loud explosions and began to run. We headed into the lights and became temporarily blinded. The wind and the snow whipped all around, and the next thing I knew, we were flying. I tried to look back and see where all our family and friends were, but the snow was blinding, and the lights were bright. I could barely see Audrey and Theodore, and I was having trouble controlling the whole flying thing. I could see they were struggling too. I was growing more and more concerned we might be lost in this massive snowstorm, and as if things weren't bad enough, the noise we had heard before seemed to have followed us into the storm. It was now screaming at us. It flashed by, all silver and shiny, and then it disappeared. When I looked back to make sure Audrey and Theodore were still with me and safe, the only one I saw was Audrey. Theodore was gone. Now all I felt was fear, the fear I had lost my boy, fear that if I didn't get myself under control, I would lose Audrey too.'

Grandma repeated Steve's story: "'I tried to slow down, and as I did, Audrey started to catch up. When she finally came alongside me, I saw the terror in her eyes.

"'Audrey yelled, "We gotta go back," and I was already making the turn. We stayed side by side and looked all around, but the snow and the lights were too much, and then we crashed. We had flown too low while trying to find Theodore; I got tangled into the trees and smashed into Audrey, and we hit the ground. The snow was deep, and it helped to break our fall. I had bumps and bruises, and my left leg was very tender. Audrey didn't complain at all. She struggled and got up and started calling for Theodore. She tried to walk around, but the snow was way too deep. I finally was able to stand up, but the pain in my leg was worse than I thought, and I went straight down. I began to yell for Theodore too, but there was no response. We called out for a long time, and finally, we both collapsed and began to cry.

"'The snow continued to pile up around us, and we began to lose hope when I heard something. I strained to make out what it was; it was far off and faint. Audrey must have heard it too because she became quiet. The sound grew louder and closer. We both began yelling for Theodore, and we kept yelling. The more we yelled, the louder the sound grew. We still didn't see anything because of the raging snowstorm, but we were filled with the hope we would be rescued.

"'The sound we were hearing was bells jingling. We finally saw a dark object in the sky, circling and circling. We kept calling out, this time for help as much as for Theodore. The dark object came closer and closer, until it began to take shape. The first thing I saw was a group of reindeer flying in formation. There were eight of them, in four rows of two, and trailing behind them was a large red object. As it drew nearer, I could tell it was a sleigh. It wasn't until they were nearly upon us that I saw a large man sitting atop the red sleigh; he seemed to be guiding it.

"'The sound of the bells grew even louder, and they continued to circle us as if they were looking for a place to land safely. Finally, they approached from our left and set down about twenty feet from us. The sleigh dug into the deep snow and stopped hard. The man atop the sleigh was thrown into a drift, and the reindeer were stuck shoulder-deep in the snow. The bells became silent, and I feared for the man and those eight reindeer.

"'Audrey called out to see if they were okay. The reindeer were checking on each other, and the man struggled to his feet. After a few tense moments, the man responded to Audrey. He said his name was Nick, and they were somewhat shook up but otherwise unhurt, and then he asked if we were all right.

"'Audrey responded first. She told him that she was sore but not really hurt, and I said that my leg hurt some but other than that, we were fine. Then Audrey asked about Theodore. "Did you see a young buck?" she blurted out in a hopeful, almost pleading voice. There was no answer. She repeated her question, and this time one of the reindeer calmly replied the storm was intense and visibility has been quite limited. He asked who the young buck was and when we had last seen him.

"'Audrey started to cry and told them that the buck's name was Theodore and he was our son. She explained what had happened on the trek and how the herd had panicked and dispersed and how the shiny silver monster making a screaming noise flashed by and caused us to get separated from Theodore.

"Steve said the man named Nick stated that was Earl, saying, 'He must have come through at the same time.' The eight reindeer nodded in agreement.

"'The large man, who had called himself Nick, began to work his way to us. It was a slow, difficult process. The deep snow was all around and still coming down and piling up fast, but he inched his way to us. It took him a long time to transverse the twenty or so feet, but he worked his way foot by foot. The eight reindeer were still harnessed to the red sleigh and were working together to try to free it from the deep snow. They weren't having much luck. Nick tried to reassure Audrey and myself everything would be fine. He said his team was the best in the world, and they would get us to safety, and when that happened, we would concentrate all of the communities' efforts on locating Theodore. His strong and confident demeanor gave us some hope.

"'That hope was short-lived. The harder the team worked to free the sleigh, the more stuck it got. Nick made his way back to the sleigh to see if he could be of any help, but the snow just kept coming, and the situation continued to get worse.

"'Audrey and I worked our way over to the sleigh while the team and Nick fought to free themselves and the sleigh from the entombing snow. Finally, Nick called for a break. Everyone stopped and took a rest. The snow continued to fall, and when our efforts resumed, the situation was even worse. Hours went by without any progress, and all the efforts had zapped the strength from the team and Nick. Nick was still trying to keep a positive outlook and giving encouragement to us and the team, but I could tell in his voice even he knew the severity of the situation.

"'The reindeer started collapsing one by one, and all we could do was rest and wait. What we were waiting for, I wasn't sure, but wait we did. The time clicked by, and hope faded. Nick continued to give encouragement and hope. He reminded the team this sort of thing had happened before, and that's why they had created a search team.

"Nick never gave up, but gradually, he began to alternate from positive words to thanking the team for all their years of friendship and loyal service. These words sounded more like preparations for final goodbyes than words of comfort and hope. Even the reindeer appeared to be losing hope. The efforts to free the sleigh had ceased altogether, and the conversations became fewer and fewer. Even Audrey was giving up. She thanked me for always being there and for the many years we had shared. She talked about Theodore as if he was in the past and seemed to be resigned. She even apologized to Nick and the team for getting them caught up in this situation and thanked each and every one of them for trying to come to our rescue.

"'Nick went to the back of the sleigh and worked with some latches. The entire end of the sleigh folded down to make a ramp. It must have been designed this way for loading and unloading, but I wasn't sure what would be loaded and unloaded into the sleigh. Whatever it was, the sleigh looked like it could hold a lot of it.

"'Nick walked down the ramp and motioned for Audrey and Me to climb aboard. Audrey fought her way through the deepening snow and climbed the ramp. I couldn't make it to the ramp because my leg had gotten worse from trying to maneuver in the heavy drifts. Nick plowed his way to me, and we fought together against the elements and finally made it to the ramp. After we were both aboard, Nick pulled the ramp back up and refastened the latches. I thanked him and Audrey, and I settled down next to them to await our fate. Nick returned to his perch and rested; I could tell he was worn to the point of exhaustion. The other reindeer, the ones Nick referred to as the team, had also settled in and accepted the dire situation we were in. One by one, the team began to lie down, and after that, nothing but silence. This was the hardest part. It was the silence that brought the full reality of the situation to a head.

"'Fear began to set in,' Steve said, 'but it wasn't so much a fear of the end, it was more a fear we would never see our families again, never see our friends, and never get to say the things we should have said all along. The silence had brought on the fear, and the fear took the last fibers of hope. This was the last thing I remembered before we all went to sleep."

Chapter 28

Grandma continued with Steve's tale: "'At the time, I wasn't sure what it was that had awoken me, but all of a sudden, I became aware something was happening. Audrey was also awake, startled out of her deep slumber. We both looked at each other and over at Nick. He too was awake and alert. The team began to stir also. The snow was letting up, and even though we were covered in it, we were all still alive and moving. What was it that had brought us all out of our state of hibernation, all at once, all of a sudden? Then I heard it, faint at first but growing steadily. It was familiar sound, sweet and strong, and it filled me with hope. Audrey began to smile, and her smile grew to laughter and tears.

"Steve said that Nick asked if it was a search party.

"'The team began talking to one another. They were taking bets on which one of the search party it was. "Thomas," one of the team announced. "I'll bet it's Thomas." Another said, "It has to be Corey or Jayme." "No way," was a reply. "It has to be Shawn or Joshua. Surely, they would be the first to find us."

"'Nick called for quiet. Again, it was completely silent, and the sound once again pierced the silence. This time it was loud and clear. It was a song, a Christmas song, and Audrey began to scream. She screamed in the direction of the sound. She screamed with joy. The song was the most beautiful sound any of us had ever heard, and it filled us with renewed strength.

"'Audrey began to sing along, and I joined in. The team was on their feet, and the sleigh moved a little. The bells jingled as they moved, and the jingling mixed with the song, and we became even stronger. We finally saw him. It wasn't Shawn or Corey. It wasn't Joshua or Jayme. It wasn't even Thomas. It was Theodore. It was my boy,' Steve said, 'and he was singing at the top of his voice. He found us; somehow, he had found us.

"'Nick seemed to sense the team was filling with renewed hope, and with this hope came strength. He seized the moment and called out to the team one by one, and they responded. The sleigh moved again, and as Theodore came closer and his voice grew louder, it strengthened the team even more, and Nick called out to the team again. The sleigh lifted into the air, and we were free from the snow. Theodore circled us, and the team launched us above the trees. Theodore had saved us,' Steve said proudly. 'His Christmas songs saved us all.'"

Chapter 29

Grandma continued, "As I was listening to Steve's story, a door opened, and Doc Brian came in. He appeared calm and turned to Steve and Audrey. He asked if they'd like to see their boy, and they headed for the door. He stopped them before they went in and informed them Theodore was very tired and weak, but with some rest and care, he should be just fine. He added Theodore wasn't able to speak very well because his voice had been severely strained somehow. Audrey let out a little laugh, and we all joined in.

"They entered the room and we followed. Theodore was lying down and having a drink, but when he saw Steve and Audrey, he tried to stand. They rushed over to him and told him to stay down and rest. He croaked out the word 'Mama,' and Audrey began crying, and then I started crying too.

"Nick was in the back of the room, and Tina went over and whispered something to him. He paused and appeared to be pondering whatever it was she said to him, and then he smiled and gave her a big nod of agreement. Without hesitating, she turned and left the room.

"Gary approached Nick after Tina left, and they talked quietly for several minutes. Nick went over and thanked Theodore for his bravery and help. He gave him a pat on the head and told him to rest and get his strength back. He said he had a great deal to do and not much time to do it, and he excused himself. At the door, he shook hands with Doc Brian and was gone.

"Gary said his goodbyes also, and I followed him to the door. He told me he was going with Nick, but he would leave Jerome and Marty with me, and they would take me anywhere I needed to go. I stayed for just one more question. The question was for Theodore, but his voice was so strained that Audrey had to answer for him. I wanted to know what everyone who had seen and heard Theodore, or Stormy, as he was known, wondered: Why did he fly all over the area in this snowstorm singing those Christmas songs?

"Stormy looked at his mother and whispered something into her ear; she looked at me and said, with pride in her eyes, 'I taught Theodore all those songs when he was very young. He was a curious and mischievous young buck and wandered off frequently. I sometimes let him get far enough away he thought he was lost. He would start to cry out in fear. I would sing a Christmas song, and he would calm down and follow my voice and return to me. As he came close enough to see me, he would join in the song, and we would both know he was all right. When we became separated after coming through the light, he said he flew all around, looking for us. He was getting scared and decided to start singing as he flew. Once he had found us, he continued to sing until I joined in, and that's when we both knew we would be all right. As it turned out, those songs not only helped us to find each other, they filled the team with strength and gave them the ability to get us all back safely.

"I could tell Stormy was growing tired, so I thanked them and left. I said my goodbyes to Kelly and Doc Brian, and headed to the sleigh Gary left for me. Jerome and Marty were ready to go. Kelly ran out after me and handed me my camera. She gave me a quick hug, and I climbed up on the sleigh and asked Jerome and Marty to take me to Tina's, and off we went.

"Tina's house looked deserted. A dim light burnt inside, but other than that, it appeared empty. I walked up to the porch and peered into the front window, but I didn't see anyone. I went around to the back and saw the canvas-covered sleigh sitting alone near the barn.

"I called out, and Todd responded. He came out and asked if I need a ride somewhere; I explained I had Jerome and Marty with me but wanted to talk to Tina for a minute. He told me she was working on a project for Nick and asked not to be disturbed unless it was an emergency.

"I let him know it wasn't an emergency and said I would catch up with her later. I went back out front and climbed aboard Gary's sleigh. Jerome asked where I wanted to go.

"I thought for a moment and told them I would like to try and find Earl if we could. They took off like a light, and we were airborne once again. We circled the town in a counterclockwise pattern. I wasn't sure how we would find him, but Jerome and Marty seemed to have a plan.

"We crossed over the candy district and flew passed Nick's place. We flew over Doc Brian's again. We covered the entire town, and as a last resort, we headed back to the plane. As we approached, I could see Eric and Kevin, hitched to the sleigh that had started my whole experience in this weird and magical place."

Chapter 30

❦

"We put down right next to them," Grandma continued, "and Marty asked them if Earl was around. Kevin said he was working in the barn. I jumped down and thanked them for the ride. I told them I would catch a ride with Earl from here, and we said our goodbyes. They were in the air instantly and were gone. As I approached barn, I could hear the sounds of tools and metal. The light coming from the inside of the barn spilled out the windows. I knocked on the smaller side entrance door. There was no answer, so I knocked again, turned the knob, and went in.

"Earl was on a ladder, bent over one of the two engines, and he was whistling a familiar Christmas tune to himself. I walked up to him and asked what was up. The wrench he was holding went flying right past my head, and the ladder wobbled back and forth.

"'Don't do that,' Earl cried out. 'You scared the candy canes out of me.' He chuckled and gave me a smile, the same smile that had kept me calm throughout this whole adventure.

"I said I was sorry and asked if the plane was all right.

"He said he was completing the preflight checklist but everything looked great, and we should be ready to go anytime. The he asked me to hand him the wrench he dropped.

"I retrieved the wrench that had zoomed past my head, and as I handed it to him, I said, 'Here's the wrench you dropped; you know, the one you dropped right past my head.' We both broke out in laughter, and he went back to work.

"I asked if there was anything I could help him with, and he pointed to a stack of boxes off to the side of the plane.

"He said it would be a great help if I loaded the boxes into the plane. They needed to take them back and distribute them to the people who had ordered them.

"I began loading the boxes into the plane. Some were larger and heavy, and some were much lighter, but they were all wrapped in brown paper and had the familiar logo printed on them in red and written in fancy old script.

"I stacked the boxes neatly on the plane. I was sure there wouldn't be enough room for all of them, but when I was finished, the plane looked half-empty. I took the straps attached to the inside of the plane's walls and pulled them across the stacks of boxes and secured them tightly. When I was done, I went and looked at my seat.

"I was planning on taking one of the unused straps left over from securing the boxes and fashioning a makeshift seat belt that would fit me better than the one I used on the trip here. As I sat down to hook my strap up, I noticed a new seat belt had already been installed, and when I pulled it across my lap, it fit perfectly. I smiled to myself, got up, and exited the plane. Earl was standing there at the door and asked if I noticed any modifications to the plane. I joked that nothing stuck out, and we shared a good laugh.

"Earl said we would need to leave tonight if we were going to get out safely. He said the plane needed a certain window of time to make the crossing out of the light barrier without sustaining too much damage. He told me we would need to be in the air within fifteen minutes of the final tree lighting ceremony at the circle. I asked when the lighting was to take place, and he said it would begin as soon as a signal was given.

"I asked him what the signal was, but he just said I would know it when I saw it.

"Earl whistled a loud piercing whistle, and I heard jingle bells, and Eric and Kevin appeared at the large barn door. They slid themselves into two straps attached to the front of the plane. These straps were similar to the ones Jerome and Marty used on the red sleigh at Nick's house. They pulled the plane out of the barn and maneuvered it around back, stopping at the beginning of the runway (which looked way too short and ended abruptly at the tree line). Earl closed the barn doors. He looked sort of sad to me, like the way Miss Penny said I looked after graduation from high school. She said, I looked like I was really going to miss that place. Ever since I arrived here, I felt like I belonged. Everyone I met instantly became an old familiar friend, and some of them even felt like family.

"Eric and Kevin climbed back into their harnesses, and Earl and I boarded the sleigh. We bolted into the sky and were on our way. We landed at Nick's place; Todd was there with Tina's sleigh. Jerome and Marty were there too. They were all still harnessed up, and it looked like they were ready to leave at a second's notice.

"The atmosphere was alive with anticipation. Earl led me to the barn, where the team was prancing nervously around in front of the large door, which remained closed. They all looked well rested and strong. Each one was wearing a leather wreath adorned with polished and shiny bells. The bells jingled and chimed as they moved about. The team gave us a nod as we walked by, and we went to Nick's office door. Earl didn't knock; he just opened the door and went in.

"All the boxes that had been in there the last time I was here were gone. Nick was at his desk, relaxing with a steaming cup of cocoa and some cookies. There were three more cups on a counter in the corner of the room and a large plate of cookies next to them. Nick offered us a mug and told me to help myself to some cookies. I thanked him and grabbed three large cookies and a mug. I was starving because I had been too busy to eat all day. Earl asked if Tina was in the back, and Nick gave him a nod. Earl grabbed the other two mugs, took several cookies off the plate, and went through the door leading to the large room where we put the red sleigh.

"Nick asked me to stay behind for a few minutes to talk. I agreed, mostly because the reporter in me had some unanswered questions, but also because the child in me couldn't help itself. Earl closed the door, and Nick offered me a chair. He took a sip of cocoa and smiled at me. He was dressed in all red velvet with a black leather belt around his large waist and shiny black boots on his feet. He wore a red stocking cap with a white fuzzy ball attached to the end of it. The white fuzzy ball hung down across the front of his left shoulder but was nearly lost in his full white beard. For me, there was no mistaking who he really was, even though no one had even hinted to it.

"Nick said, 'Well, it seems you've had quite an adventure since your arrival. I trust you still have some questions you'd like answered. We don't have much time before you leave, but I will answer any that I can.'

"I pondered for a moment and asked my first question: 'Where and what is this place?'

"He explained, 'This place is our home. This is where we live and work and share our lives. It isn't much different from any other place, except for maybe the flying and talking reindeer thing. We just want to live a productive life and spread a little joy and some of the Christmas spirt along the way. What do you think this place is?'

"I said that based on what I was told my entire life, I'd say this was the North Pole. This was where Santa Claus lived with a bunch of flying reindeer and elves, who made toys for good little girls and boys. If I was going to guess what this place is, I would say it was Christmas Town. Nick didn't say anything else, but he nodded and smiled.

"My second question was a follow-up to the first one. I asked Nick straight up if he was Santa Claus, who travels the entire world on Christmas Eve and delivers toys to the good little girls and boys, who rides in a red sleigh pulled by eight reindeer and wears a red suit and has a white beard, the one some cultures also call St. Nick.

"This one made him chuckle. His smile grew, and his cheeks flushed. He composed himself and answered cautiously, 'It sure sounds like you are describing me. But legends are built on small bits of truth. One of those truths is that I travel in a red sleigh pulled by a team of reindeer, but as for the name Santa Claus, this could have come from someone catching a glimpse of the sleigh as it was leaving and reading the "S A N T A" logo displayed on the back. This logo is just the logo of the company Earl and I worked for before we came here. We bought the sleigh to help haul some of the equipment we bought to start our own company. This truth is a base for a story, and as it is with any story, the more times it is told and the more people who tell it, the bigger it grows. After a while, the story takes on a life of its own and then grows some more. Each piece of the truth is stretched and twisted to meet the needs or desires of the one who is telling it. If it is told often enough and by enough people, it becomes their version of the truth. Because of this, some consider me to be the one you call Santa Claus, but my given name is Nicolas Clousen.'

"Once again, Nick neither confirmed nor denied my question and left it up to me to decide. So I thought I would try to pin him down with my next question: 'What about the St Nicolas thing?' I asked. 'If you're not St. Nicolas, then why is it written on a sign on your street?'

"The laughter became much stronger this time. He nearly couldn't contain himself. When he calmed down, his answer was the simplest of all: 'It's not St. (Saint) Nicolas; it's St Nicolas. The *St* is an abbreviation for *Street*. Street Nicolas is what it is. Where Earl and I came from, the streets and roads were labeled that way. It was just the way we spoke and wrote back there.'

"I said that made sense, but what about the list, the one with the good and bad children on it? I told him I saw the boxes containing names on the plane and in his office.

"He said, 'Those are not lists of good and bad children; those are lists of people of all ages who either have the Christmas spirit or have lost it. We get these names from parents or friends or family members concerned their loved ones are losing the Christmas spirit. We use the list to try to find a way to give them this spirit back. This is what we do on Christmas Eve. It isn't just toys to some children; sometimes, it's as simple as a fly over with the sleigh and the jingling of the bells. Also, before you ask, not everyone has a chimney, so make out what you will about that part of the legend.'

"The last thing I wanted to know was how this could go on year after year, decade after decade, for hundreds of years, without anyone getting older or passing away. As a reporter, I felt it was my duty to ask this one.

"Finally, I asked how he was able to travel the whole world in one night.

"Nick looked at me with a twinkle in his eye. I was sure he was going to give me some story about magic, or time warps, or something I wouldn't be able to understand, but instead, he asked me a question. He asked if I believed in the Christmas spirit.

"I just shrugged my shoulders and said, 'I guess so.'

"He said, 'The Christmas spirit is more about trust and faith than it is about understanding why and how. Many people think they know the whys and hows, but only a few still have the trust and faith. This is why most of the people in the world who still have the Christmas spirit are young children. They don't focus on the whys or the hows. As for an answer to your question, tell me something: Have you noticed something different about this place? Have you found anything odd here since you arrived?'

"I thought about it for a moment. Several things came to mind immediately.

"I told Nick the first thing I noticed was there were no clocks anywhere. Even my own watch didn't work. The next thing that came to mind was how the whole town seemed to do everything in a counterclockwise pattern. The streets run counterclockwise, the reindeer all fly in a counterclockwise direction, and everyone uses a counterclockwise motion when they mix anything. For example, the cocoa is always stirred in a counterclockwise direction, as were the chocolate, the cookie dough, and the fudge.

"Nick said that was good and asked if I noticed anything else.

"I said I had never seen the sun, or the moon, for that matter. The only changes of light or dark were caused by the northern lights. They shimmer and glimmer but never seem to go away.

"Nick said, 'Miss Jane, where you are from, time is everything. People are always worried about what time it is. They worry about being late or even too early. When the sun comes up, they get up and start their day, and when the sun goes down, they believe the day is done. Because of this obsession with time, it passes them by, and they grow older, a day at a time. The days add up to weeks, the weeks to months, and finally the years pass them by, and they barely notice it's happening until their time is up. When my brother and I first arrived here and met the reindeer, we were shocked they could fly and talk. They were the ones who taught us about time. They showed us how to slow the effects of time down by moving in a counterclockwise direction and focusing on the moment and not the time of day or week or year, and this is why you never see a clock around. We incorporated this motion into our daily routines, and it allows us to live every moment in itself. This ability to slow the effects of time is how come they are so fast, and it is their speed that enables me to traverse the entire world in one night. Time still passes us by, but at a different rate. We grow older like everyone else, just at a greatly reduced rate. Even your watch is still moving forward, but it is happening so slowly, it appears to have stopped. What has felt like days to you since you have been here has really only been a few seconds. Finally, the sun and the moon are just timekeepers themselves. The northern lights block them out, and without seeing them, we are not forced to abide by their ways.

"He added, 'This is how it is for children. Children tend to feel time passes much slower than adults do. To a child, summer feels like it lasts forever, and Christmas doesn't last just a day or a week, but all year long, but as we grow older and the worries of time and life begin to weigh people down, they begin to lose their Christmas spirit. When this happens, they try to recapture glimpses of it through the children, the same way our parents did, through traditions.'

"And with that, the impromptu interview was over. Nick said it was almost time to go; he stood up, finished his cocoa, and headed for the back door. I finished my cocoa and followed him. We entered the large room where the red sleigh had been housed after Gary and I cleaned it. The room was empty except for the sleigh, Tina, Gary, and Earl.

"Gary was on the sleigh, looking over the mountains of packages that had been loaded onto it since the last time I saw it. There must have been hundreds or maybe a thousand of them, and they were wrapped in colorful, shiny paper, and they all had a small tag with a name on it. The only space on the sleigh left open was the seat right behind where the team would soon be hitched.

"Nick approached the sleigh and inspected it just like Earl inspected the plane before he deemed it ready for flight. He checked the runners (the things I was calling skis), he checked the latches that held up the back of the sleigh where it folded down to a ramp, and he checked the harness, soon to be occupied by the team of eight strong and proud reindeer.

"He seemed satisfied, gave Gary an approving nod, and asked Tina if she had everything ready. She smiled and told him everything was ready and in place.

"The final thing Nick did was to walk over to Earl and reach out a hand to him. Earl took the hand and pulled the big man in close and gave him a hug. No words were exchanged between the two, but none were needed."

Chapter 31

❦

"Earl walked straight to the large door at the front of the barn," Grandma continued, "and with one pull, it was full open. The team stirred anxiously as the door opened, and without any prompting, one by one, they took their places in the harnesses. Gary made one last check of the harness and gave Nick a thumbs-up with his big red mitten, and the sleigh began to move.

"Out into the glow of the bright northern lights, the sleigh emerged from the barn, and the rest of us followed. Gary and Tina made their way to Tina's canvas-covered sleigh, where Todd was ready to go. Earl motioned me to join him on Gary's sleigh.

"We climbed up, and as soon as we were seated, Eric and Kevin launched us into the air, and we were off. Jerome and Marty appeared to our right, and I couldn't help myself; I shot them a big smile and gave them the queen's wave. I heard Jerome let out a big laugh and saw Marty just shake his head. The snow had begun once again; this was one of the happiest moments of my life.

"We circled the roundabout, and I could see the entire town was assembled. I could hear a cheer rise up above the jingling bells, and we swooped in and landed in the midst of the crowd. Tina and Gary landed right next to us, and another cheer went up. Earl jumped down from the sleigh; Tina and Gary were already on the ground and making their way to the decorated tree in the center of the circle.

"I scrambled down and stood for a moment, not knowing what I should do; Earl turned to me and gestured for me to join them. I felt privileged and humbled all at the same time, but I followed him anyway. I noticed something that made me pause before I joined them in front of the tall center tree. The very top of the tree was covered with a brown mesh bag, the same type of mesh bag I had seen on the trunk of Tina's tree, the bag which held the dirt that kept the tree alive until it was replanted after the season has passed. Attached to this bag was a rope, and the rope ran down the tree. Tina walked up, stood next to the tree, and took the rope. The snow started to pick up some more, and the northern lights reflected off each and every flake. I looked around, and once again, it was like a million diamonds floating softly from the sky.

"I heard the jingling of bells ringing in the air and knew they were the bells from the team. Everyone looked to the sky, and seemingly out of nowhere, they appeared. Another cheer erupted from the crowd, and this one was almost deafening. The team put the sleigh down directly in front of us as the crowd continued to cheer. Nick stood up on his sleigh, and the crowd quickly became quiet.

"He began by saying, 'Welcome, my friends. I want to thank you all once again for your hard work this year and your support of each other. I want to be honest with you; there was a time recently the team and I didn't think this day was going to happen.'

"Everyone bowed their heads, and now it was completely silent. I felt tears well up in my eyes, and then Nick continued, 'We were stranded and became weak and had all but given up. We knew every one of you were doing all you could to find us, but the storm was greater than any of us had ever experienced before. We said our goodbyes and decided whatever happened, we were fortunate to have been able to do so much over the years, and if had to end, at least we would be all together. I believed in my heart that no matter what happened, Earl would find a way to keep the company going, and you would continue supporting each other until the time our special gifts and works were no longer needed. Just when things appeared to be over, an outsider came to our rescue. This outsider gave us a gift, and his gift was the power of love. His love for his family pushed him to risk his own life to save his family, and his gift came in the form of song. His Christmas songs were so beautiful and so filled with love and selflessness, they gave us a strength even we didn't know we had. It was because of this strength and selflessness Tina approached me earlier with a suggestion while we were at Doc Brian's. As you may have guessed, the individual I am speaking about is none other than Theodore.'

"The crowd once again roared. I saw Theodore standing up near the front next to Kelly and Doc Brian with his parents, Steve and Audrey. He looked embarrassed by all the attention, but his parents couldn't have looked more proud. He was much taller and appeared older than I remembered him as he crossed the sky, singing all those Christmas songs just days before.

"Kevin started a chant: 'Stormy, Stormy, Stormy,' and soon everyone joined in. I even caught Earl and Nick chanting along, and this made Theodore blush and smile all at the same time.

"Nick raised his hands, and the group quieted down; he continued, 'We could never repay Theodore or Stormy, as you like to call him, for his courage and persistence. I truly believe without him, the team and I would not be here with you today, so to try to show our thanks [Nick motions for Stormy and his parents to step forward which they reluctantly did], we have decided to bestow on him our highest honor.'

"At this point, Nick looked over at Tina and gave her a small nod. Tina grabbed hold of the rope attached to the bag on top of the tree and gave it a tug. The bag fell off the top of the tree, and in its place was a statue of Theodore, standing proudly atop the tree. Around his neck was a leather collar, and engraved into the collar was the name 'Stormy.' It was colored in red and written in the old script writing. The red ink was mixed with flakes of gold and silver, and as the northern lights reflected off of it, the name glowed, as if it was illuminated with a bright light. The whole town broke out in applause, and the chanting started up again: 'Stormy! Stormy! Stormy!'

"As the chanting echoed into the trees and beyond, another sound began to build. This sound started as a low rumble and built steadily until it overtook the chants. This sound was approaching from the right, and everyone stopped and looked that way. I was beginning to become afraid, but as I looked around, everyone else looked like they were happy and excited to hear it. Earl took my hand, and Nick sat back down in the sleigh. The sound was almost directly above us at this point; I could feel it vibrate through my entire body, and if it wasn't for Earl holding my hand, I think it would have knocked me over. Then the sound was gone, and following it was a bright light streaking from right to left in the sky. As it passed overhead, the entire area lit up like a spotlight was shining directly onto the statue of Stormy. Everything glowed, and a halo surrounded the entire circle; just as quickly as it came, it was gone.

"Earl leaned down and whispered that it was time. He began to lead me to toward Gary's sleigh, and Tina followed. The crowd stood there as if they were waiting for something. As we reached the sleigh, Nick turned to the group and said, 'May the spirit of Christmas be with you, now and forever more,' and with that, the red sleigh began to move. It rose into the air and circled the entire group. Nick gave one last wave, and the team, the red sleigh, and Nick simply disappeared in the direction of the streaking light.

"It was completely silent at this point, and no one moved; it was like being frozen in time. The silence was finally broken by a single voice, Stormy's voice. It started softly, like the sound of an angel. As it grew, other voices joined in. The voices blended and strengthened until it was as if an entire choir had joined together in one final song of songs. 'Silent night, holy night,' they sang, and it was right at that moment I knew I was changed forever. I felt like a very young child experiencing the true spirit of Christmas for the first time. I couldn't move, and the tears flowed uncontrollably. Earl said he was sorry, but we had to go now. He helped me into the sleigh, and Tina handed me my camera bag.

"She gave me a tight hug and said, 'You might need this," and walked away with tears in her eyes.

"Gary climbed in beside me, and with Earl on my left and Gary on my right, the sleigh took flight. We flew faster than I even knew was possible. Within seconds, we were back where it all started, back at the barn and back with the plane.

"The plane was sitting outside the barn; Earl jumped down and walked directly to it. Gary turned to me and said it was time for Earl and me to go. He too gave me a strong hug, and then he climbed out and helped me down. He grabbed my bag and handed it to me, and we followed Earl to the plane. I stopped and turned back to the sleigh; I ran back and gave both Eric and Kevin a big hug, and with tears in his eyes, Kevin told me to take care of myself. Eric cleared his throat a couple of times and said in low voice, 'Come back and visit us sometime, anytime.' He turned his head away, and I thought I heard him sniffle a little. I began to cry myself and hugged them both one more time, and then I turned and ran to the plane.

"The door was open, and the first of the two engines was cranking over. Gary was waiting for me and helped me into the plane. I stopped at the top step and turned to say goodbye, but as I opened my mouth to tell him thanks, the engine fired up, and he couldn't hear me. He must have known what I was going to say because he winked, waved, and mouthed the words, 'Miss you,' before closing the door.

"I made my way to my seat, and the second engine fired up; both were running smoothly. Earl turned from his seat and handed me my headphones. I set my camera bag down and pulled out the video camera, turned it on, and checked the battery level and available tape time left. With a full battery and forty minutes of tape left, I set it on the seat next to me and put on my new seat belt. It fit perfectly, and I snugged it up. I noticed the seat pad was new too, and it was almost comfortable.

"I put on my headphones and said, 'Check, Earl, do you have a copy, over?' He turned and smiled and responded, 'I read you loud and clear, Miss Jane. Hang on tight, over,' and with that, he gave me the thumbs-up signal and eased the throttles forward. We began to move. Out of my window, I saw Gary, Eric, and Kevin for the last time. I gave them a short wave, and they disappeared from my view. I had to take a deep breath, and we left the barn behind us as we stopped at the end of the runway.

"Earl's voice boomed, 'Here we go,' through my headphones, and the engines roared to full life. I grabbed my video camera, pointed it out the front window, and hit the Record button. The plane lurched forward and steadily gained speed. There were a few bumps as we picked up speed, but I kept the camera as steady as I could. The tree line was approaching quickly, and once again, I had my doubts we would lift off in time to clear the treetops. We were speeding directly at the wall of evergreens, and just when I was sure we were at the point of no return, Earl pulled the yoke of the plane all the way back, and we were off the ground. We climbed slowly at first, and then, at the last possible second, the plane lifted, and we somehow missed the trees, and I realized I wasn't breathing. I took a deep breath and exhaled and turned the camera to my side window and continued taping. The plane banked to the left, and we did a long, slow counterclockwise turn as we continued to climb. When we finally leveled out, we were right above the main circle of the town, and I zoomed in on the tree in the center. I was hoping to get a final view of the statue of Stormy adorning the top of the tree, and as I did, the entire time I had spent here rushed through my mind. The faces of all the people and reindeer I had met were etched into my memory forever. It had only been a minute or so since we took off, and I could still see the town in my lens, but I was already missing them all … and this magical place.

"We quickly were out of view of the town and headed directly to the edge of the northern lights. The lights grew brighter with every second that passed. Earl's voice filled my ears once again. 'We are about to enter the lights,' I heard him say. 'It's going to be real rough for a while, so brace yourself, over.'

"I replied, 'Check, I'm ready! Over.'

"The snow continued to pick up, and he turned the wipers on. It was as if we were returning into the same storm we had left just days before. The plane began to bounce, and I took the camera from my face and just pointed it out the windshield. When we first entered the edge of the lights, the plane smoothed out, and I thought to myself, *This isn't so bad,* and then it was. It felt like we hit a wall and the plane was going to break apart. I could no longer hold the video camera, so I just pushed it down on the seat next to me. The snow became blinding, and the wipers were going full blast. I was having a hard time focusing because the plane was shaking so violently. I could make out Earl fighting the wheel, and the engines roared to full power. They were so loud that even with the headphones on, the noise was almost deafening. Fear began to well up inside of me. The lights outside filled the plane and began to blind me; I felt like I was spinning. The noise of the engines and the bright flashing lights started to make me feel woozy again, just like I was before everything went black the first time. I started feeling warm and beads of sweat began rolling down my forehead into my eyes. I used the sleeve of my parka and mopped the sweat off my head and out of my eyes, but it wasn't sweat. My sleeve was bright red again, and right then and there, I knew it was blood, my blood. I felt sick and started seeing sparkles before my eyes. It reminded me of the reflections of the lights bouncing off the falling snow, the million softly falling diamonds. Things were now growing dark, and the last thing I remembered before I completely blacked out was Earl turning back to look at me. The last thing I saw was the grave fear displayed in his eyes."

Chapter 32

"The first thing I remembered," Grandma went on, "was the smell; even before I opened my eyes, I knew what the smell was. It was strong and distinct. It was the smell of disinfectant, and the not household cleaner-type of disinfectant; this was the real deal: hospital disinfectant. I wasn't sure how or why, but I was in the hospital.

"I tried to think back to the last thing I remembered. I searched my mind, and the harder I tried, the more my head hurt. I could hear the beeps and clicks of the machines running around me, but I was just too afraid to open my eyes. As I searched my mind, I remembered the assignment to film the reindeer migration in Alaska for WXMAS, the TV news station where I worked. I remembered setting up a trip to Alaska with Susan, the station's receptionist, and I remember buying a white parka and some white rubber boots. The next thing I remembered was getting off a plane in Fairbanks, meeting a man named Earl, sitting in a diner with a waitress named Heather, and a cozy cabin in the woods, with a fireplace and hot cocoa and cookies. I also recalled flying in Earl's little silver cargo plane and filming the reindeer. I remember seeing the flashes on the ground, the reindeer scattering in all directions, and the plane dropping from the sky, the pain above my eye and blood, and that's all I remembered. I passed out again.

"The next time I woke up, I still smelled disinfectant and heard the machines beeping. I instinctively raised my right hand and felt my head, just above my right eye. There was a thick bandage wrapped around my head. As I touched the cloth, all the other memories came flooding back to my mind. I began to remember the lights, the talking and flying reindeer, and the cocoa and cookie shop. I even remember the decorated trees standing in front of the log houses. I remembered Gary, Tina, Nick, the red sleigh, and the team that pulled it. Last but not least, I remembered Stormy. Stormy, the singing reindeer who crossed the sky all day and night.

"I finally decided it was time to open my eyes. I had to see if Kelly would be there, or Doc Brian, or at least Earl. I opened my eyes slowly, and the room was dark. My vision was blurry. I blinked a few of times, and things started becoming clearer. As I regained my focus and my eyes adjusted to the darkness, I was filled with disappointment. This was a real hospital room. I was in a real hospital, and I was hurt, and I was alone. There was an IV in my left arm, and it dripped a clear liquid from a bag hung on a metal pole next to my bed. The liquid flowed down a tube and into my arm. I could see a door behind it, partially open, and a white light reflected off a mirror above a sink against the wall. In the mirror, I could see a shower with the curtain half open, and next to it, a toilet, and I knew it was the bathroom.

"Next to my bed, on the right, stood a small metal table with two drawers, and on it sat a red plastic poinsettia. Hanging from the rail on the left side of my bed was a rectangle box with a white cord running down beneath the bed and out of sight. The box had two blue switches. Each switch had two arrows, marked UP and DOWN. I reached for the box and pressed one of the switches marked UP and heard the sound of an electric motor. My feet began to rise, so I released the button and pressed the DOWN arrow, and the motor lowered my feet. I pressed the UP side of the other button, and the motor sound started again, and my head began to move. I raised my head until I could see the entire room. This made my head hurt; I became dizzy and thought I would pass out again, but I took a deep breath and fought it off. I looked at the box and saw a red button with the word CALL printed on it and pressed it. Nothing seemed to happen, so I pushed it again, and within a few seconds, the door directly across from me opened, and bright white light spilled into the room. The light caused my head to hurt even more. I had to squint and blink to try and adjust to the abrupt change in lighting. I saw the silhouetted figure of a woman wearing a dress, standing in the doorway.

"She said, 'You're finally up,' and the door closed behind her, and the darkness returned to the room. I could see she was dressed all in white, and a stethoscope was draped around her neck. 'My name is Nurse Cally,' she said. 'How are you feeling?' She approached me, took the stethoscope from around her neck, and put it to my chest. She told me to take a deep breath and then another. Next, she took out a thermometer and put it under my tongue. She took my pulse and shined a light in my eyes, one at a time. After removing the thermometer and reading it, she wrote something on a clipboard hanging off the end of my bed.

"She asked if I needed anything, and I told her I was thirsty. She opened the top drawer of the metal table with the poinsettia on it, took out a blue plastic cup and a small pitcher with a lid on the top, and walked out of the room.

"The light flooded the room once again, but this time, I was able to keep my eyes open, and my head barely hurt. Nurse Cally returned with the pitcher full of ice and water, filled the blue cup, and handed it to me. I took a few sips and finally asked her where I was. She told me I was in the hospital in Fairbanks. I was getting ready to ask her how I got here and what day it was when she stopped me and told me Dr. Bryant would be in soon to answer any questions I had. Before she left, I asked if I could use the bathroom; she nodded and showed me how to get out of bed and move the pole with the IV bag to the bathroom.

I was a little dizzy when I stood up, but it quickly went away. She stood with me as I walked to the bathroom, and when she decided I was steady and safe, she left the room.

"I looked into the mirror and saw the bandage. I touched it and felt the lump. I could feel the stiches under the wrap, and that's when I remembered hitting my head on the frame of the plane's window. I remembered the warm, red liquid running down my face and seeing it on my white parka. Once again, my memories changed to flying reindeer and the sleighs. I was feeling confused.

"I came out of the bathroom and stopped at what looked like a closet; I opened it and saw my parka and rubber boots. The parka still had bloodstains on it, but it looked as if someone had tried to clean them. I saw my camera bag and opened it; all my equipment was there. My clothes were hung next to my coat, and my suitcase was packed and setting on the ledge at the bottom. I started to feel weak, so I returned to my bed to lay down and shut my eyes. I began to have visions of the Great Northern Christmas Spirit & Tree Co. I could see all the people and reindeer. I saw all the decorated trees, and I could even hear the songs of Stormy. Was it all just a dream? Did I just imagine the whole thing? Could I have been in a dream-filled coma? I began to cry.

"The door to my room opened once again, and Nurse Cally came in, followed by a man. He wore a long white coat and also had a stethoscope hanging around his neck.

"He looked at the clipboard at the end of my bed, smiled at me, and said, 'Good evening, Miss Jane; looks like you're doing much better. My name is Dr. Bryant; I was working when you came in. You had quite a nasty bang and gash above your eye, and we had to put a number of stiches in it. We gave you some pain meds and an IV with antibiotics and fluids. You weren't showing any signs of a concussion, so we let you rest. Once the pain meds wear off, you should be able to leave. I'm going to write you a prescription for pain medication and an antibiotic. I want you to take the pain medication as needed and finish all the antibiotics; any questions?'

"I had a million questions, but I wasn't sure how to ask them, and I didn't want to sound crazy, so I started with, 'What day is it?' Then I asked, 'How did I get here?'

"Dr. Bryant got a page on the intercom and excused himself, but Nurse Cally stayed back and answered my questions. She began with what day it was. She said today was December nineteenth; she must have seen the shock on my face because she asked if something was wrong.

"I told her that wasn't possible, because the nineteenth was the day I had gone with Earl on his plane to videotape the reindeer migration, and she said that it sounded right to her because an older man named Earl was the one who brought me in. Maybe it was the pain meds still affecting my mind, but I know I was at the Great Northern Christmas

Spirit & Tree Co. with Earl till late in the evening on the twenty-first. Again, I began to wonder if all of this was just a dream. Tears welled up in my eyes, and Cally asked me again if I was okay. I shook my head and said I was tired and just wanted to rest. She told me she would be back later. As she left the room, I asked if she could call Earl for me; she told me he didn't leave a number to contact him, but he said he'd be back later to check on me.

"The next time I opened my eyes, it was because something had drawn me from my sleep. It wasn't a noise or a flicker of light; it was another smell. I could smell cocoa. It was sweet, and it made my mouth water. It was mixed with the scent of fresh baked cookies. I turned to the metal table next to my bed, and in the place where the plastic poinsettia had sat was a plate of cookies and a large mug of cocoa. I smiled and sat up. I noticed the IV was out of my arm, and the metal pole was gone. There was a small cotton ball taped over the place where the tube had run into my arm. My head was clear, and even though I still had a bandage above my right eye, the pain was gone.

"I took the mug of cocoa and brought it to my lips. I gave a light blow across the top and cleared the steam rising from it, revealing eight miniature marshmallows floating on the top, in four rows of two. I took my first sip and picked up a tree-shaped cookie from the plate. It was still warm, and when I took my first bite, it was perfect. I ate all four cookies and downed the mug of cocoa and felt all the strength return to my body. I got out of bed, retrieved my clothes, and went into the bathroom to put them on. As I was coming out of the bathroom, the door to the hallway was open, and Earl was standing there. He was wearing a smile, but his eyes had the look of worry in them.

"He said he was glad to see me up, adding that I gave him quite a scare. He said, 'I'm sorry about letting you get hurt; I was just trying to save the reindeer.'

"I walked over to him, gave him a hug, and told him I understood. He said I was released to go home anytime I wanted and that he would give me a ride to the airport. He said if we left now, I could still make my flight home and beat the big storm.

"I told him I was ready and put on my parka and boots. Earl grabbed my camera bag and equipment, and we headed for the parking lot. The snow was coming down pretty hard at this point, but we climbed into his old pickup truck and headed to the airport. I decided not to ask him anything about the Great Northern Christmas Spirit & Tree Co. or red sleighs or flying, singing, or talking reindeer. We just rode in silence. At the airport, he stopped at the curb and climbed out of the truck. I got out, and he handed me my stuff; we looked into each other's eyes. All I could say was 'Thank you,' and he hugged me. As I turned to go inside, I took one last glance back, and he gave me that comforting smile of his, and I saw a tear roll down his cheek. I heard the truck pull away as I entered the airport, and that was the last time I saw him."

Chapter 33

The sadness in her voice made me sniffle. Grandma had a tear rolling down her cheek, and my dad had left the room. I could hear him blow his nose as he walked out. At this point, I was wiping my eyes, and before I could say anything she began again.

With a catch in her voice, she said, "I checked my luggage and picked my ticket up at the counter, and the ticket agent said I had just made it in time. She said this would probably be the last flight out today and maybe the last one before Christmas. She said a major storm was coming, and within the hour, the whole airport would be shut down. She pointed me to my gate and told me to hurry. I ran, partly because I was worried I wouldn't make the plane and partly because it was the only way I could relieve the grief I felt about not seeing Earl again.

"I got in my seat by a window, and they closed the door. I heard the engines come to life and buckled my seat belt. I was the only one in my row, and as the stewardess came by to check I was buckled in, I heard a familiar voice say, 'Welcome back.' It was Nichole, and she asked about the bandage on my head. I shrugged it off with a smile.

"We took off without incident, and even though it was bumpy at first, we flew away from storm, and it smoothed out. This flight would bypass Anchorage and go directly to Minneapolis and I was almost glad to leave Alaska behind. I fell asleep, but no dreams accompanied my sleep this time. I awoke as we landed in Minneapolis. I changed planes for the relatively short trip back to Detroit.

"Back in Detroit, I retrieved my luggage and took a shuttle to my car. I drove back to Indiana and went straight to the TV station. I pulled into the parking garage, and Scott the security guard met me at the door; he welcomed me back and made a comment about the bandage on my head and the bloodstains on my parka. I smiled and told him I would catch him up later.

"I went straight to the editing room and shut the door. I locked it, turned the 'In Use' sign on so no one would disturb me, and pulled out my video camera. I ejected the tape and put it in the edit machine. I hit Rewind, and when it stopped, I looked at it and hesitated. I was wondering if when I played it, I would see the town. I wondered if it would contain video of sleigh rides and flying reindeer. I hit Play, and the first images were from Earl's truck and North Pole, Alaska. After that came the footage of the plane lifting off from Earl's house over the trees, and it was as scary as it looked to me when it happened. There was some footage of moose and also a good view of some polar bears next to a lake. After that was the reindeer, migrating all in a line. The video was spectacular. The northern lights danced alongside the reindeer. The video took a violent turn, and then I caught the flash from the hunters' guns. I captured the reindeer scattering, and then the lens hit the window of the plane, and there was a brief shot of Earl looking back at me. The next thing on the tape was the floor of the plane and the red and green boxes. Lights filled the video, and there was a long pause. The video picked up again with the plane over the scattering reindeer, and it ended.

"I was so disappointed. If there was such a place where reindeer talked and flew, apparently I was never there. It was all just a dream brought on by a head injury and pain medications. I sat for a long time and then did what I was trained to do. I edited the video and took all the parts out that didn't pertain to the migration. I added a voiceover describing the scene, and with only fifty-seven seconds of useful footage, I took it to John.

"I handed him the tape, and he asked about the bandage on my head. I waved it off, and he played the tape. He didn't say a word, but when it was done, he rewound it and played it again. He looked up at me, smiled, and said, 'Perfect.' He thanked me and said it would air on the five o'clock time slot on Christmas Eve and again at eleven. He thanked me again and told me to go home, get some rest, and take care of the bump on my head."

Chapter 34

Grandma continued, "I left the station and drove back to my apartment. I went to bed and slept till noon the next day. When I woke up, I changed the bandage on my head, and while it was off, I looked at it for the first time in the mirror. It was going to leave a nasty scar; I knew right then and there I would never be an anchor on a TV news show because the scar would be too distracting for the audience.

"I did a lot of thinking the rest of the day, and my thoughts went back to when I was a little girl at Christmastime at my parents. I packed a bag and left the next morning for home.

"It was the day before Christmas Eve, and when I opened the front door to my parents' house, the smell of pine needles hit me first. It smelled like Christmas. I could smell cookies baking in the kitchen, and Mom let out a yell when she realized I was there. The tree was perfect, and my dad gave me a big hug. We baked cookies and listened to Christmas music on the radio, and it was good. I couldn't help but think back on my dream of the Great Northern Christmas Spirit & Tree Co., but I never brought it up to anyone.

"The next day was Christmas Eve; we sat around the tree and shared stories of Christmases past. We opened our presents at midnight because that was how we did it at my parents' house; it was our tradition. Once the gifts had all been unwrapped, and I was ready to retire for the night, my dad stopped me. He said there was one more. He said he wasn't sure who left it, but he had found it on the front porch just before I arrived. He handed me the note that accompanied it. The note was folded in two, and when I opened it, I let out a gasp. It was handwritten, in old script with red ink, and simply said, 'May the spirit of Christmas be with you, now and forever more!'

"I began to cry. I couldn't stop myself. Mom rushed over and gave me a hug, and Dad asked who it was from.

"I wiped the tears from my eyes, and a smile came upon my face; all I could say was, 'Some of my dearest friends.'

"Dad said to open it; I sat down in front of the tree and carefully removed the colorful paper. After I removed the wrapping, it revealed a wooden box with the words 'The Great Northern Christmas Spirit & Tree Co.' engraved on it and colored in red ink. I opened it up and pulled out a wooden figure of a young reindeer. Around his neck was a leather collar, and it simply read 'Stormy.'

"I cried out in joy, and it startled my parents. They must have thought that I was crazy when I asked my dad if we could remove the star at the top of the tree and put this wooden reindeer in its place. He looked at my mom and shrugged his shoulders. He went into the kitchen, got the stepstool from the closet, and took the star down. He climbed off the stool, looked at me, and nodded.

"I put that reindeer tree topper on the highest bow, stepped down, and plugged it in. The collar lit up, and the tree began to glow in its red light. Just then, I heard the jingling of bells, and that's when the tradition began."

Chapter 35

I was once again crying, but this time, it was tears of joy. Grandma's story had changed me. I couldn't wait for them to light the tree. The front door opened, and my uncles, aunts, and cousins all started to file in. "Merry Christmas" was shouted from each and every one as they entered. I heard my cousins saying it smelled like Christmas in here, and Dad went in the kitchen and started pouring cocoa for everyone.

After everyone had a mug, we gathered around the tree; Grandma stood up and said, "This year, Brandi will have the honor of lighting the tree." To my surprise, everyone began to clap, and for the first time in my life, I felt I was ready for this great honor. I wasn't any older, and I certainly wasn't an adult, but I was different. For the first time in a long time, I could really feel the spirit of Christmas. I plugged the cord in; the tree lit up, Stormy lit up, and it was more beautiful than I ever remembered.